HEARTWARMING INSPIRATIONAL ROMANCE

*Love Inspired*®

# Hannah's Courtship
## Emma Miller

Hannah's
Daughters

LARGER PRINT

# Love Inspired®

**Uplifting** romances of faith, forgiveness and hope.

## AVAILABLE THIS MONTH

**HANNAH'S COURTSHIP**
*Hannah's Daughters*
Emma Miller

**SINGLE DAD COWBOY**
*Cooper Creek*
Brenda Minton

**SECOND CHANCE SUMMER**
Irene Hannon

**THE BACHELOR MEETS HIS MATCH**
*Chatam House*
Arlene James

**LAKESIDE SWEETHEARTS**
Lisa Jordan

**UNEXPECTED REUNION**
*Southern Blessings*
Carolyn Greene

ISBN-13: 978-0-373-81768-9

5 0 6 7 5

S EAN

LILPATMIFC0614

# "Hannah, will you walk outside with me?" Albert asked.

"Albert, I—" She...what? What was she going to say to him? How could she explain her flustered behavior? "Albert, I should..."

"Hannah, don't talk. I need you to listen to what I have to say before I lose my nerve."

They were standing by the gatepost, within arm's reach but not touching. She raised her head and looked into his eyes. For an instant, she felt the jolt of his intense gaze. And then, before she could react, she got a face full of raindrops as another shower swept over them in a drenching wave.

Albert grabbed her hand. "Quick!" he said. "Into the truck!" He dashed across the yard, pulling her with him.

Hannah's heart was suddenly pounding. He was holding her hand! She knew that it was wrong, but it was impossible to break free. Laughing, she threw caution to the wind and ran after him. She didn't care about the rain, didn't care who could be watching, didn't care if she was breaking every rule she'd lived by for more than thirty years.

**Books by Emma Miller**

Love Inspired

*Courting Ruth*
*Miriam's Heart*
*Anna's Gift*
*Leah's Choice*
*Redeeming Grace*
*Johanna's Bridegroom*
*Rebecca's Christmas Gift*
*Hannah's Courtship*

*Hannah's Daughters

## *EMMA MILLER*

lives quietly in her old farmhouse in rural Delaware amid fertile fields and lush woodlands. Fortunate enough to be born into a family of strong faith, she grew up on a dairy farm, surrounded by loving parents, siblings, grandparents, aunts, uncles and cousins. Emma was educated in local schools, and once taught in an Amish schoolhouse much like the one at Seven Poplars. When she's not caring for her large family, reading and writing are her favorite pastimes.

# Hannah's Courtship
## Emma Miller

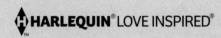

**⬥HARLEQUIN**®LOVE INSPIRED®

If you purchased this book without a cover you should be aware
that this book is stolen property. It was reported as "unsold and
destroyed" to the publisher, and neither the author nor the
publisher has received any payment for this "stripped book."

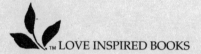

Recycling programs
for this product may
not exist in your area.

™ LOVE INSPIRED BOOKS

ISBN-13: 978-0-373-81768-9

HANNAH'S COURTSHIP

Copyright © 2014 by Emma Miller

All rights reserved. Except for use in any review, the reproduction
or utilization of this work in whole or in part in any form by any
electronic, mechanical or other means, now known or hereafter
invented, including xerography, photocopying and recording, or in
any information storage or retrieval system, is forbidden without
the written permission of the editorial office, Love Inspired Books,
233 Broadway, New York, NY 10279 U.S.A.

This is a work of fiction. Names, characters, places and incidents are
either the product of the author's imagination or are used fictitiously, and
any resemblance to actual persons, living or dead, business establishments,
events or locales is entirely coincidental.

This edition published by arrangement with Love Inspired Books.

® and ™ are trademarks of Love Inspired Books, used under license.
Trademarks indicated with ® are registered in the United States Patent
and Trademark Office, the Canadian Trade Marks Office and in other
countries.

www.Harlequin.com

Printed in U.S.A.

All these blessings will come on you and
accompany you if you obey the Lord your God.
—*Deuteronomy* 28:2

# Chapter One

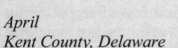

*April*
*Kent County, Delaware*

Heart thumping, Hannah Yoder awoke with a start in her bed, barely catching her Bible before it tumbled off her lap to the floor. Still foggy with sleep, she placed the Good Book safely on the nightstand beside her bed and retrieved the reading glasses that must have fallen when she dozed off. *What time was it?* Glancing at the clock on the mantel over the fireplace, she saw that it was eleven-thirty.

*I'm getting old and foolish,* she thought, *falling asleep with the propane lamp on.* She never did that. A mother with a houseful of children had to be vigilant against accidental fires…especially when they lived in a two-hundred-year-old house.

And then she remembered that five of her girls

were grown and married and the sixth was promised to the community's new preacher. *Where has the time gone? Only yesterday, I was a young woman with a husband and seven beautiful children, and today, I'm widowed and nearly fifty.* In another month, there would be only her youngest daughter, Susanna, and her foster son, Irwin, left to share the big farmhouse.

Nearly midnight and she had to be up by five-thirty…She'd never been one to have trouble sleeping, but maybe the stress of preparing for Rebecca's wedding was affecting her more than she realized. She reached up to turn off the lamp, but then a nagging uneasiness tugged at her and drew her from the bed. The floorboards were cold and she slid her bare feet into a pair of her late husband Jonas's old fleece-lined slippers and reached for her flannel robe.

Something didn't feel right. What had awakened her? Had she had a bad dream? One of her windows was open a crack, letting in a cool, damp breeze, but that wasn't what had raised goose bumps on her arms. No, something was amiss.

She went to the window and stared out into the night. All was quiet in the farmyard. Common sense struggled with maternal instinct. Neither of the dogs had raised the alarm. True, their old sheepdog was somewhat hard of hearing, but

Irwin's terrier could hear a mouse squeak in the next county. There was certainly no intruder. What troubled her?

Hannah had always considered herself a calm, rational woman. One couldn't remain sane raising a houseful of children and be prone to nervous fancies. She looked back at her bed, wanting nothing more than to crawl back under the covers and get a good night's sleep. But she knew that she wouldn't get a wink until she'd reassured herself that all was well.

Taking a flashlight from the nightstand, she switched it on. Nothing. Not even a faint glow. The batteries were dead. Again. Hannah sighed, guessing that Susanna had been playing with it.

The propane lamp was attached to the wall, so she took an old-fashioned kerosene lantern from the top of a dresser, lit it and, holding it high, padded into the hall. Quietly, feeling silly, she opened first one door and then the next. There was nothing out of place in the spare bedroom across from hers. No one in the downstairs bathroom. Green eyes peered back at Hannah from the settee in the parlor, and her heart skipped a beat.

*Meow!*

"Oscar." She let out the breath she'd been unconsciously holding. "Sorry." The glowing green orbs blinked and the tomcat flattened his single remaining ear against his gray head and flicked his long tail back and forth, obviously annoyed at being disturbed when he was on duty.

The landing at the bottom of the main staircase was still, every item in place, the wood gleaming and free of dust. And no wonder, Susanna, the same careless daughter who'd used up the flashlight batteries, had spent all afternoon waxing the floor and furniture, polishing the oak balusters and steps, and sweeping away cobwebs.

A smile curved Hannah's lips. Dear, precious Susanna, born with Down syndrome. Twenty-one and forever a child. Whatever Susanna did, she threw her whole heart and soul into it. That daughter, at least, would remain home with her. In spite of the challenges of mothering a special child, Hannah had always thought of Susanna as God's gift, much more of a blessing than a worry.

The kitchen, warm and cozy from the fire in the woodstove, was as tidy as Hannah had left it when she'd gone up to bed at nine. Irwin's shoes stood on the steps that led to the back stairway. Hannah opened the door to the staircase and smiled again. From the second floor came the loud, regular buzz of Irwin's snoring. Hannah held the lantern up higher and called softly. "Jeremiah!"

She heard the patter of small feet, and the face of a scruffy terrier appeared at the top of the stairs. "It's all right, Jeremiah," she said, closing the door. If Jeremiah was on guard, no one had come unbidden into the house. She checked the back door, found it locked and retraced her steps to the front room. She'd found nothing to cause her concern, but she still wasn't satisfied.

*I'm being ridiculous.* "I should just go back to bed," she said, her voice louder than she intended. But she wouldn't be able to sleep until she'd fully investigated the house. She started up to the second floor where Rebecca and Susanna slept. Susanna's room first. Empty, as expected. Susanna had wanted her own bedroom because, in her own words, she was a woman grown. But, usually, she grew lonely at night and crawled into her sister's bed.

The bathroom door stood open, the interior dark. The unused bedrooms presented a wall of closed doors, all latched from the hall side. No problem there. There was only Rebecca's chamber left, where Hannah expected to find both of her girls fast asleep. It was a shame, really, to disturb them by opening the door and shining lamplight into their eyes. She did it anyway.

*"Mam?"* Rebecca stirred and raised a hand to shield her eyes. "What time is it? Did I oversleep?"

Hannah stepped into the room. Rebecca was alone in the four-poster bed. No Susanna. "Where's your sister?" she asked, trying to keep the alarm out of her voice. "Where's Susanna?"

"In her bed, I suppose." Rebecca rubbed her eyes with the backs of her hands. "She never came in. I thought—"

"Are you sure?" Hannah raised the lamp to see into the far corners of the room. "She's not in her room."

"Downstairs, maybe? Sometimes she gets hungry and—"

"Not in the bathroom. Not in the kitchen." Hannah suppressed a shiver. "She's not anywhere in the house."

Rebecca scrambled out of bed and found her robe. "I don't think she'd go outside. She's afraid of the dark. She's got to be here. Remember the time we thought she was lost and we found her asleep in the pantry?"

Hannah grimaced. "She was eight years old, and she was only missing for a little while. I went to bed at nine. I don't know how long she's—"

"We'll find her." Rebecca pulled on a pair of black wool stockings and took her sneakers out of a chifforobe. "You check the house again. I'll look in the yard and barns." She turned on a high-powered flashlight. Hannah was glad to know that Rebecca's still had batteries.

Another search of the house, including the rooms over the kitchen, where Irwin slept, proved futile. Anxiously, Hannah stepped out onto the back porch. Rebecca, identified by the bobbing flashlight beam, was just coming out of the barn. "Is she there?" Hannah called.

*"Ne."* Not Rebecca's normal tone. Her voice was flat.

Hannah's fear flared. Rebecca might not have found Susanna, but she'd discovered something she didn't like. "What is it?" Hannah demanded, coming down the steps to the back walk. She hurried to the gate, gripping the gatepost to keep her balance. "What's out there?"

"It's what's *not* there, *Mam*. The pony's gone. And Dat's courting buggy."

Hannah stared at her. It was too dark to make out the expression on Rebecca's face, but what she could make out from her tone confirmed Hannah's alarm. Sensible Rebecca was as frightened as she was. "Susanna took the pony and cart," Hannah said.

Rebecca gripped her mother's arm. "Where would she go in the middle of the night?"

Hannah didn't have to think twice. "David's."

David King, the only other person with Downs syndrome Susanna had ever met, was the apple of her eye. For months, Susanna had insisted that she *loved* King David, as she called him, and that she was going to marry him.

The Kings didn't live far away, only a quarter of a mile from the end of the lane and to the right, on the opposite side of the county road. But Susanna wasn't allowed to leave the farm alone, and she'd never driven a horse and buggy. Hannah hadn't thought that Susanna could even hitch the pony to the cart. And to be out at night, going down a road that carried trucks and cars? Hannah shuddered, and prayed that God would watch over her.

"We'll find her," Rebecca said. "She's fine. I'm sure of it. We haven't heard any ambulances. You know how the dogs bark when a siren goes off. Wherever she is, Susanna is fine."

"She won't be when I catch up with her," Hannah pronounced. Of all of her girls, Susanna was the last one that she had ever suspected would sneak out at night to see a boy. Johanna, maybe Miriam, or even Leah, but not Susanna. Susanna was an obedient daughter who always followed the rules. It had never been her youngest daughter that had given Hannah her few gray hairs... until now.

"Do you want me to hitch up Blackie?" Rebecca asked. "I'm not dressed, but—"

Hannah set her jaw. "I'm going to walk to the King's house."

"In your bathrobe?"

"We have to find her." Hannah tightened the tie on her robe. "Every minute counts, and I trust the Lord will forgive me for my state of undress. Give me your flashlight."

"I should go with you."

"No, you stay here," Hannah told her, taking the flashlight. "Just in case she comes back and I miss her."

"I'll light the lamps in the kitchen." Rebecca went one way. Hannah another.

The dirt farm lane was a long one, and usually Hannah was grateful that her late husband had picked a place where the house was set far back off the road. Tonight, however, she wished it were a shorter driveway. *Oh, Jonas,* she thought. *Why aren't you here with me?* In the five years since a sudden heart attack had taken him from her, she often wished he was still here by her side, but never more so than tonight. She wasn't a weepy woman, but if she had been, she'd be inclined to sit down in the dirt and have a good cry.

She walked quickly, not bothering to call Susanna's name. If she was coming up this lane, with or without the pony and cart, Hannah would have heard her. Instead, all she heard was the far-off wail of a freight train and the high chirping and deep bass croaks of early spring frogs.

The lights of a car whizzed past Hannah's mailbox. Not far now. The Kings' farm was dark. As with all the Old Order Amish in their community, David's parents didn't have electricity. Hannah had been hoping for the gleam of a kerosene lamp through an uncurtained window, but not a single glimmer showed.

Hannah's anxiety increased with every step. "Susanna," she murmured. "Where are you?" If she wasn't at the Kings' house and she wasn't on the road between here and there, Hannah would have to wake her sons-in-law and maybe send Irwin to the chair shop to use the business phone. Calling the English authorities wasn't a decision to be taken lightly. If an eight-year-old Amish child had been missing at night, it would be considered acceptable. Though Susanna might technically be twenty-one, her maturity level was closer to that of a second-grader.

At the end of the lane, a grove of cedar trees blocked her line of vision on the right. There was no moon tonight, and even with the flashlight, it was difficult to see. Hannah had just turned onto the shoulder of the road when she saw a bobbling light a few hundred feet away. "Susanna?" she called. No answer. Hannah called again. "Susanna!" *Please, God,* she prayed silently. *Let it be her. Let her be safe.*

Whoever it was, they were coming slowly, and Hannah couldn't hear hoof beats or the grate of buggy wheels on the pavement. She hurried toward the light. "Susanna?"

*"Mam?"*

Relief jolted through Hannah with a physical impact. She broke into a run. "Susanna, are you all right?"

"She's fine!" came a reply in a deep male voice. "I'm fine."

That was Susanna's voice, but who was with her? Hannah stopped short and aimed the flashlight toward the approaching group: Susanna, short and round, bouncing along in her flat-footed, side-to-side stride and a larger, lumbering figure behind her.

A pickup truck approached, slowed and passed. In the glow of the headlight, Hannah saw a third person, a tall Englisher in a baseball cap leading Hannah's black-and-white pony. No, she decided, not just any Englisher. She recognized that voice. "Albert Hartman? Is that you?" She started toward them again, not running this time, but walking fast.

In another moment, she had her arms around a sobbing Susanna. Her daughter was trying to tell her something, but she quickly dissolved into hysterics. Because Susanna's speech was never clear to begin with, Hannah had trouble understanding what her daughter was trying to tell her.

"Crash," David supplied. He was a young man of few words. "Bam," he said. "Ina ditch."

Hannah gazed over Susanna's head. "Are you

hurt, David?" she asked. "What about Taffy? Is the pony—"

"Not a scratch, so far as I can tell. It could have been a lot worse."

Hannah accepted Albert's opinion without hesitation. Not only was he a longtime family friend, but he was a local veterinarian. She turned her attention back to her daughter. "Why did you go out at night?" Hannah demanded. "And what made you take Taffy?"

"Pizza," David said. "We wanted pizza." He shook his head. "*Mam* gonna be mad at me. *Ya.*" He nodded his head. "Really mad."

"I was so worried. Come on," Hannah urged. "Let's get off this road before we're all killed." She held tight to Susanna, unwilling to let her go now that she'd found her. Adrenaline still pumped through Hannah's veins, and she felt vaguely sick to her stomach.

"Good idea," Albert said.

Together, they walked back to Hannah's lane. Once away from the blacktop, she loosened her grip on Susanna's arm and merely held her hand. "Albert," Hannah said, "how did you find them? *Where* did you find them?"

"Half a mile on the other side of the Kings' place," he said. "I was coming back from a call. A cow having twins was in a bit of trouble. Two pretty little heifers, both right as rain once we got their legs untangled and got them delivered. Anyway, I was just on my way home when I saw Jonas's courting buggy in the ditch and these two standing there beside it."

"A car came," Susanna wailed. "It scared Taffy. She jumped in the ditch."

"The buggy rolled over on its side," Albert explained. "A wheel is broken, but the carriage seems okay. I was more concerned for Susanna and David."

"Not David's fault," Susanna stoutly defended. "He drove good. The car beeped and scared Taffy."

Hannah rolled her eyes. "David drove?"

Susanna nodded.

They continued to walk up the long drive. "But, Daughter, you snuck out of the house."

Susanna shook her head. "*Ne.* I didn't."

"You did," Hannah said. "Did David come to the farm and hitch Taffy to the buggy?"

"*Ya,*" Susanna said, but David was shaking his head. "Hush," Susanna ordered, shaking her finger at him. "You *said!*"

Confused, Hannah glanced at Albert, who shrugged. "I couldn't get a straight story out of them, either. They were both crying when I got there. The pony was tangled in the traces."

"It was God's mercy that you found them," Hannah said. The pony belonged to her daughter Miriam, but she stabled it at the home barn so that Rebecca and Hannah had the use of it. They were all very fond of Taffy, and the thought that the animal could have been badly injured or killed by Susanna's carelessness made Hannah angry. "I'm disappointed in you, Susanna," she said sharply. "Very, very disappointed."

Susanna hung her head. Tears ran down her cheeks and she wiped at them with dirty hands, but Hannah wasn't feeling sympathetic.

"What you did was wrong and dangerous," Hannah chided. "You, David or Taffy could have been killed."

"We…we wanted pizza," Susanna mumbled. "You never…never let us go get…get pizza."

"I like pizza," David declared.

The sound of an approaching horse and buggy caught Hannah's attention. "That's got to be Rebecca," she explained to Albert. "Where's your truck?"

"I left it on the side of the road by the buggy."

Hannah nodded. "I can send Charley and Eli to get the buggy in the morning."

"No worry," Albert said. "I called Tony's Towing."

"But that will cost dearly," Hannah said. *Did she even* have *the money for a tow truck?*

"Don't worry about it." Albert gave her a reassuring grin. "Tony owes me for stitching up his Labrador's hind leg last week when he got it caught in the screen door. There won't be a charge. He'll have the buggy back in your barn within the hour."

Rebecca reined in Blackie, and Susanna pulled away from Hannah to run and tell her sister about her adventure. David stood patiently where he was, waiting for Susanna or someone to tell him what to do.

Hannah glanced back at Albert. "You walked right past David's house. Why didn't you leave him there?"

Albert tugged off his ball cap and looked sheepish. "He wouldn't go. Susanna wanted him with her, and I thought maybe you'd be uneasy about me bringing her home alone. You know, how it would look to the community…"

"How it would look? When you saved both of them from who knows what? Albert, you may not be Amish, but we trust you. You'll never know how grateful I am that it was you who came along when I needed you most."

"I suppose it was meant to be," Albert offered slowly. "His plan. I'm just glad I could help."

Rebecca climbed down out of the buggy, and Hannah quickly filled her in on what had happened. "We'll tie Taffy to the back and take her to the barn, and put Susanna to bed," she continued. "Albert and I are going to walk David home—"

"No need for you to put yourself out." Albert started to lead the pony around to the back of the buggy. "I can take David home."

"*Ne,* Albert," Hannah replied. She gave Susanna a gentle push in Rebecca's direction. "I need to come. David's mother has to know what he was up to. I don't think she'll be any more pleased with this night's mischief than I am."

# Chapter Two

❧

*All I need now is for Bishop Atlee to drive past and see me walking down the road after midnight in my bathrobe and house slippers—accompanied by two men*, Hannah thought wryly.

She supposed the wisest thing would have been for her to go back to the house and get dressed, but that would have taken more of Albert's time, and the Yoder family had already put him out a great deal tonight. Her oversize wool scarf and dark blue, ankle-length bathrobe covered more of her than her everyday dresses. She might not be conventionally garbed for an Amish woman, but no one could say she wasn't decently covered.

She was sure that Albert, a Mennonite born-and-bred, with more than the usual allotment of sense for a man, would understand her stretching the rules of proper dress due to the emergency. After all, wasn't Albert practically a member of the family? His nephew, John, was married to her daughter Grace.

Albert had been a friend and veterinarian to the Seven Poplars Amish community for many years, and as long as Hannah had known him, he'd always treated her with the greatest respect. To put a fine point on it, Albert treated her as an equal, as a person with a brain in her head. She was certain that Albert wouldn't be ashamed to be seen with her under these circumstances.

It was a short walk from her mailbox to the driveway of the Kings' farmhouse. Only one motor vehicle passed them, a small car, not the tow truck that Albert had called to bring the disabled buggy home. She and Albert kept their pace slow enough for David, who was often distracted and had to be reminded to stay on the shoulder. David never did anything quickly, and any attempt to hurry him would have triggered upset and possibly tears. Hannah had no wish to deliver him to his parents in an emotional dither.

Hannah liked David, and she liked his mother and father. They'd done a good job raising him, and she was sure that he'd never given them reason to think he'd sneak out with a girl to go to Dover. Tonight would be an awakening for the Kings as much as it was for her. David and Susanna, who had always been obedient, had suddenly become problem children.

Fifteen minutes later, Hannah and Albert were back at the spot where Hannah's driveway met the road. David was safely in the care of his parents, and everyone had agreed that nothing good would come from trying to hash this mess out tonight. Albert had insisted on walking Hannah home, although that had felt silly. She was a woman in her late forties, a schoolteacher and a mother who'd been managing her farm and her affairs for years. She was certainly capable of following her own lane back to her home without an escort.

"Call me old-fashioned," Albert said, trudging along beside her. He hadn't been put out by her objection. If anything, he sounded amused. "I just wouldn't feel right if I didn't see you safely to your door." When she didn't answer, he went on. "It's not the same world we grew up in, Hannah. You read the papers. All kinds of craziness going on."

"I try to stay away from the world as much as possible," she replied. It was what her Amish faith taught. *Be not of this world.* The Amish were a people apart, living not so much for today as for their future in heaven.

Albert was a member of the Mennonite Church, another Anabaptist sect that shared a long history with the Amish. The two faiths had separated before they came to America in the eighteenth century. The Amish believed that the Mennonites were too worldly, and Amish founders felt it necessary to remain separate. Today, the Mennonites did charity work with the general public and spread their religion through worldwide missions. The Amish kept to themselves and did not evangelize.

Hannah herself had been born and raised in the more liberal Mennonite faith, but she'd become Amish when she married Jonas Yoder. Although it had cost her dearly, she'd never regretted her decision.

"Wickedness," Albert continued. "Riots, bombings. People using violence against their neighbors."

"I hardly think there's going to be a riot in my farmyard tonight," she teased. "My sister-in-law Martha isn't all that fond of me, but I doubt even she wants to harm me. And my other neighbors are my daughters, my sons-in-law and my grandchildren, so I feel pretty safe."

"You hear stuff on the news every day. I can't help but worry."

"Maybe you should stop listening to the radio and watching television."

"Evil happens."

*"Ya,"* she conceded. "It does. The best we can do is to live according to our conscience, treat one another as the Bible teaches us and pray that God will see to the rest."

"I suppose." Albert was a middling-size man, broad shouldered, with a sturdy body, chestnut-brown hair and a pleasant face. Usually, he walked with a vigorous stride, making him seem younger than his fifty-odd years, but since his father's death two months ago, Albert had lost the spring in his step.

Hannah and most of the Amish community had attended the funeral, and everyone had noted how hard Albert had taken the elderly man's passing. It was natural, she supposed. Albert had never married, and he and his father had lived together ever since Albert had joined the veterinary practice. Maybe Albert was lonely, Hannah thought. John had moved out when he finished building his new house, and now Albert lived alone. His days were full of work, but maybe he missed having someone at the supper table to swap stories with.

"Don't tell me you aren't worried about Susanna," he said. "I know better. You're a woman who's always put her children first. I've always admired that about you, Hannah, that you are such a great mother. And the way your girls turned out proves that you did most things right."

Hannah's throat tightened and she concentrated on the beam of light on the ground in front of them. Rebecca's flashlight was a good one, and it was easy to follow the hard-packed gravel drive. For the first time, she felt a little uncomfortable around Albert. She wasn't used to discussing private matters with outsiders. Although he'd proven himself to be a good friend to both her and her late husband, this subject was awkward. "I do worry about Susanna's future, naturally," she admitted stiffly. "But I have to trust in God's plan for her."

"You think He has a plan for each of us?"

"Of course." She was so surprised that she stopped walking and stared at him. "Don't you?" She knew that Albert was a faithful member of his church, and she'd assumed that he felt the same way.

"Sometimes I think so. But sometimes…"

She heard him exhale slowly.

"Sometimes I wonder if God spoke to me but I didn't listen… If I've waited too late to do what I should have done years ago."

She pressed her hand against her midsection to keep from touching him. Albert was obviously distressed. Had he been one of her children or sons-in-law, she would have reached out to him to touch his shoulder or take his hand, but they were alone. It wasn't proper that she have physical contact with a man not related to her. "In what way?" she asked. "How do you feel that you failed?"

He went on, not directly answering her question. "Getting through college was hard for me. I didn't want to borrow money, so I worked two jobs and attended classes full-time. I never had time for dating. And, then when I got into vet school, it was a struggle for me to keep up my grades."

"And after you graduated? Did you think of marriage then?" Standing outside the circle cast by the flashlight, Albert was a dark, indefinite figure. Hannah knew that she was intruding on his privacy, but out of compassion, she persisted.

"I tried to make up for lost time. I went out with different women, but I was too focused on my veterinary practice. I just wasn't ready to settle down."

"And now you regret not marrying and having children?"

"I think when a man hits fifty, he begins to realize that this is it. His life is more than half over. I've always loved taking care of animals, but there's something missing in my life."

"Have you talked to your preacher about this? Or to John?"

"No."

She and Jonas had wondered why a good man like Albert had never married. Among the Amish, a man or woman remaining single was almost unheard of. She remembered that some time back, before Jonas had died, Albert had kept company with a lady dentist in Dover. The couple had often gone to fund-raiser breakfasts and school auctions together. But, then, Jonas had come home one day and said that the Englisher dentist had married. Not Albert Hartman, but a lawyer.

Not knowing what to say, Hannah walked on a short distance until she came to the edge of the farmyard. "We're here," she said, "and it looks pretty quiet. No rioters." She smiled at him. "I really appreciate what you've done for me—for Susanna—tonight."

He stood there a moment. "I suppose I should get back to the buggy. The tow truck will be there, and the driver might need help loading it." He glanced toward the house. "You can lock up. I'll see that he delivers the buggy. No need for you to wait up."

Hannah found herself yawning. She nodded. Tomorrow was a school day, and she'd have to be up early. Before she left, she'd have to confront Susanna, and she wasn't looking forward to that. "Thanks, again, Albert. I don't know what would have happened if you hadn't helped."

"Don't say another word. Like I said, Hannah, I'm just happy that I came along when I did."

Leaving Albert by the gate, she went into the house. Rebecca and Susanna had already gone up to bed. She returned to her bedroom, removed her robe and slippers, and knelt in prayer. If there was ever a night that she needed to give thanks to God, this was it.

\* \* \*

Because it was overcast and threatening to rain when she left home in the morning, Hannah didn't take the shortcut across the pasture to the Seven Poplars School as she usually did. Instead, she hitched up Blackie and drove the family buggy. Teaching twenty-six children in eight grades in one room wasn't easy, but she'd been doing it for five years.

When Jonas had suddenly died of a heart attack, she had not wanted to have to rent out her farmland or sell off any acreage. She'd known that a woman with six girls and no menfolk couldn't make enough off the crops to survive, so she'd convinced Bishop Atlee and the church elders to allow her to take the open schoolteacher's job.

Teachers were usually young single women, but Atlee had thought highly of Jonas, and he'd agreed. Hannah had been thankful to be given the opportunity, and she'd always believed that Atlee Bontrager's decision had been influenced, at least in part, by his fondness and admiration for Jonas.

The school had been a good fit for Hannah. She loved the challenge of teaching, and she loved the children. An added bonus was that being so close to home meant that she could keep a close eye on her own family while working. The pay in the church school wasn't much, but it was enough to provide independence for Hannah and her daughters. Having a steady income was the reason that she'd gone against custom and had remained unmarried after the usual period of mourning had passed.

The day turned out to be an unusually hectic one. She sent Joey Beachy home at noon when he'd thrown up on the playground. She'd asked Irwin, who was Joey's cousin, to walk the child back to the Beachy farm. Naturally, Joey had walked to school that morning, but it had been with his brothers and sisters, and Hannah hadn't felt right sending him home alone. Irwin was delighted. Hannah doubted that she'd see him again until suppertime. Her foster son didn't like school, and ensuring that he received a standard education had been her cross to bear.

She gave a math test to her combined fifth and sixth-graders, and directed rehearsals for the program done every year for parents and friends. Naturally, none of the boys had memorized their parts, and the walk-through for the skit had ended in tears when two sisters each wanted the same role. Hannah was glad that it was a busy day, because it gave her less time to worry about what she would say to David King's parents.

As soon as the last child had departed at the end of the school day, Hannah drove directly to the King house. Though she still had to contend with a tearful Susanna at home again, it seemed wisest to first discuss the incident with David's mother, Sadie. That way, the two mothers could present a united front. Something had to be done. David and Susanna couldn't go on pretending that they were walking out together.

All the way there, Hannah hoped that Ebben, David's father, would be out of the house. This was women's business, and having Ebben be part of the conversation would make it more awkward for her. Sadie was a good, loving mother and a fine friend. Surely, she and Sadie could put an end to this behavior without harming either of their children.

"Come in, come in." Sadie must have been watching for her because the stocky little woman came out the side door as soon as Hannah drove up the lane. "Ebben!" Sadie called. "Take Hannah's horse." And then to Hannah, "Let Ebben see to him. You come in and have some of the applesauce cake I just took out of the oven."

Sadie's kitchen was smaller than her own, but just as clean. Simple white linen tiebacks hung at the windows, and pale yellow walls brightened the room. A round oak table with four chairs stood in the center of the room. Overhead hung a white kerosene lamp decorated with faded red roses, lit now against the gray afternoon.

"Tea?" Sadie asked. "Or coffee?"

"Coffee, if it's no trouble," Hannah responded.

Sadie bustled around, reminding Hannah of a banty hen in her gray dress, black stockings and white *kapp* and apron. Sadie's clothing still reflected the Amish community that they'd lived in before they'd moved to Delaware. Her *kapp* was sewn slightly different, her skirt and apron were longer and she wore high-topped black leather shoes, rather than the black canvas sneakers most women in Seven Poplars wore in the summer.

Sadie poured the coffee and brought a tiny pottery cream pitcher and matching sugar bowl to the table. She sliced generous pieces of applesauce cake and placed them beside the coffee mugs. "Honey or sugar?" she asked. "I like raw sugar, but Ebben and David do love that honey your Johanna brought us at Christmas."

Hannah was eager to see what David's parents thought about the previous night's misbehavior. Still, it would have been rude to jump right into the subject. First, news of children's and grandchildren's health and activities had to be exchanged, and Hannah had to tell Sadie about the plans for the school picnic. Sadie asked what Hannah was bringing for the shared meal after morning church service on Sunday, and when Hannah said potato salad with peas, Sadie wanted the recipe.

Hannah forced herself to at least appear relaxed, but she couldn't help glancing around.

Ebben remained outside, and there was no sign of David. "David's outside with the chickens," Sadie said as she refilled Hannah's coffee cup. "Would you like another piece of cake?" Hannah shook her head. "David loves chickens," Sadie continued. "Ebben says he can coax two eggs a day out of those hens. David's a good boy."

Hannah nodded. "I know he is."

Sadie's right hand trembled as she reached for the sugar. She clenched her fingers into a fist and buried it in the folds of her starched apron. "He's a sweet boy, Hannah, a really gentle soul."

Hannah murmured in agreement. "So is my Susanna."

Sadie knotted her fingers together. Her faded blue eyes grew misty with tears. "When David was born, the midwife told me that he was a Mongoloid."

Hannah winced. The term was wrong. Ugly. *"Downs,"* she corrected softly. "With Down syndrome. Like my Susanna."

"She wasn't Amish. The midwife. 'He might not live,' she said. 'A lot of times babies like him have a bad heart. It might be a blessing if he did—' My Ebben, he's quiet, like David. But he got so mad at that woman. 'Don't you say that!' he said. 'Don't you say such things about our beautiful son.' And he was beautiful, Hannah. He had this mop of yellow hair, as yellow as May butter, big blue eyes and the sweetest look on his face."

"My husband always said that Susanna was a blessing from God."

Sadie nodded eagerly. "Ebben asked that midwife to leave and not come back. We took David to a baby doctor at a big hospital. He told us that David would grow and learn like any other child. But he never said what a good boy David would be. He's never been willful." She hesitated. "It's why we never thought that David would ever…"

"Sneak out at night?"

"Our older son, now that one. When he was *Rumspringa*—he was a caution. Sowing his wild oats, Ebben always said. And if David wasn't… didn't have Downs, we would have expected him to…"

"But he does. *They* do." Hannah swallowed against the tightness in her throat. "We've always protected Susanna, kept her close. She's afraid of the dark. Running off to buy pizza…" Hannah exhaled softly. "I don't know what to do. They just have this idea that—"

"That they're courting," Sadie finished. "I know. I know it's crazy, but David is very fond of your Susanna. He talks about her all the time."

"They could have been killed in that buggy accident."

"I know. I couldn't get a wink of sleep last

night. David's driven in the field and in the yard, but never a horse on the road. He doesn't understand the danger of motor vehicles. It's a blessing your pony wasn't injured when the buggy went into the ditch."

Both women were quiet for a moment.

"The question is," Hannah said, "what do we do about them? I almost sent her to Brazil to visit Leah and her husband. I thought that maybe a few months away from David and—"

Sadie cut her off absently. "He was sick. When he was little. Cancer. We thought we were going to lose him. But God was good. The doctors…"

She raised her gaze to meet Hannah's. "He can't ever be a father, our David. The doctors said it's impossible. Some boys with his…with Downs… But for certain with David. He'll never be able to…you know."

"Oh." Hannah almost said she was sorry, but was she? Was that a blessing, considering David's difficulty in taking care of his own needs? And why was Sadie sharing that? What did it have to do with Susanna and David sneaking off at night?

"I was just thinking," Sadie said. "Ebben's cousin's daughter Janet, she's slow. Not Downs. Not like Susanna or David. But she can't read, can hardly count to twenty. David can, you know.

He can read, too. Easy books and *The Budget*. He loves to read *The Budget* to us in the evenings."

Hannah waited, wondering what Sadie's point was.

"Janet, she got to an age where she wanted to be like her sisters, wanted to walk out with boys and go to the singings and the frolics. And pretty soon, she had herself a beau."

"What did her parents do?"

"They talked to their bishop and their church elders, and they all decided that the best thing to do, considering…"

Hannah shifted in her seat. "Was?"

"To let them get married."

*"Get married?"* Hannah repeated.

Sadie nodded.

"Are you suggesting that—" Hannah stopped and started again. "Are you saying that you think that David and my daughter—" She took a moment to compose herself. "Sadie, Susanna and David could never be married and live alone. They could never live a *married* life."

Sadie pressed her lips together. "Maybe not the same married life we've had, but…" She looked down at her hands, then back up Hannah. "I'm not saying we should give them permission to court. I just think it's something we need to keep in the back of our minds."

# Chapter Three

Albert pulled into the long driveway that led through the trees to his nephew John's new log-cabin-style home. He glanced at his watch as he pulled into a spot in front of the porch. He was right on time.

He'd had a good day, considering that he'd had less sleep last night than usual; by the time he'd returned from the Yoder farm, it had been after two in the morning. Not that he minded. As a matter of fact, he'd enjoyed the little adventure. Of course, he was concerned for Hannah's daughter and her friend. Thankfully, everyone was safe. No harm done.

And his day had turned out to be an easy one. Besides the four routine calls for immunizations, he'd stitched up a pig's snout, and done a physical examination on a nice-looking colt. With the new vet that he and his nephew had hired tending to the small-animal portion of the practice, he was free to spend his time where his heart was, with large-animal cases: cows, horses, pigs, sheep and goats.

John and his wife, Grace, stepped out onto the porch and waved. Albert felt a rush of pride. He'd never fathered a child, but John was as close to being a son as a man could ask for. And the wife he'd chosen, Grace Yoder, had come to the marriage with a bright-eyed little boy who had eased his way into Albert's heart.

Albert walked around the truck, opened the passenger door and let his dog out. From the floor, he took a bag containing a junior-size pair of binoculars he'd found while poking around in his attic. They had been John's when he'd been around Dakota's age, and he thought the boy might like them.

"Come in, Uncle Albert," Grace called. "Supper's ready. My spaghetti and Johanna's yeast rolls. Your favorite." She led them into the house and the dog trotted behind them. "She sent them home with me when I went to pick up 'Kota."

"Where is the little rascal?" Albert looked around. "I brought him these." He held out the binoculars.

"He's not here," Grace explained. "Johanna invited him to stay overnight with Jonah, and I couldn't pry him away."

"He'll be sorry he missed you. But I know he'll love these. I remember when Gramps bought the binoculars for me," John said, taking them from Albert and peering through them. "The two of us used to go bird-watching on Sundays after church."

"I'll just finish up in the kitchen," Grace said with a smile. "You two catch up on vet talk." She hurried away, auburn ponytail swinging behind her.

Albert grinned at John. "I like that girl more every time I see her. You picked a winner. I'm just going to wash up." He pointed toward the half bath in the hall.

John bent to pat the dog's head. "I did, didn't I?" he said. "Grace has made me happy, really happy."

Albert paused at the bathroom door. "You'd have to be crazy if you weren't happy, with her and 'Kota."

Albert entered the small room, switched on the light and closed the door behind him. Funny, he thought as he soaped his hands, how much life there seemed to be inside the walls of this house. He looked into the round mirror. "Love inside these walls," he murmured half under his breath. For days, he'd been looking forward to sharing this evening meal with the three of them. Home was pretty lonely without Pop there now, just him and old Blue and the two cats that had somehow wormed their way into the family.

Blue had been a hard-luck case just like the cats, and had turned out to be one of the best snap decisions he'd ever made. Not a lot of people wanted a three-legged coon hound that couldn't hunt anymore, but he and Blue suited each other just fine. Without Blue… Albert sighed. Dogs had short lives, compared to humans, but most folks couldn't help getting deeply attached to them, and he'd be the first to admit he was guilty.

Grace was still in the kitchen when he joined John at the long pine table in the dining room. As she had predicted, they each had stories of the day's patients and their owners to share. Albert settled into a chair, took a sip from the glass of iced tea John had given him and studied the spacious room.

The log walls, the heavy log beams and wood floors gave the place a real flavor, and Grace and John had furnished it with a mixture of vintage pieces, such as a beautiful refinished icebox and a scarred church pew, mixed with a few antiques. Nothing was fancy. So far as he knew, the young couple didn't own a television. Other than the laptop, which lay on a maple desk in the living room, and electricity, the house could have been from another century.

"So what's this I hear about you coming to the Yoders' rescue last night?" John asked.

"Amish telegraph?" Albert asked with a chuckle.

John laughed. "Johanna told Grace. I can't imagine Susanna and David King out on the road at night with a pony. It's a wonder something worse didn't happen to them."

Albert leaned back in the chair. "I came along at the right time. Whoever ran them into that ditch kept going. But it might teach those kids a lesson and keep them out of worse trouble."

Grace came to the table with individual bowls of garden salad. "Susanna's never done anything like that before. I've never known her to get into any kind of trouble. She's such a sweet girl."

"You think it's serious, David and Susanna?" John asked Grace. "They seem to spend a lot of time together."

"I don't know," she answered.

"It worries Hannah," Albert said. "We got to talk some when we walked David back to his house. You've got to admire Hannah for the job she's done with your sister. It can't have been easy. David's parents, too. From what I've seen of him, he seems like a good boy. But Hannah's alone. She's had to go through all this dating and courtship stuff with all of her girls all by herself since Jonas passed away."

A timer went off in the kitchen. "That's the

pasta," Grace explained. "Supper's coming up as soon as I can drain them."

"Is the buggy a total loss?" John asked.

Albert shook his head. "No, not at all. A new axle should fix it good as new. Hannah was fortunate in that, too."

"That's great," John sipped his tea. "Buggies are expensive, and I know the family thinks a lot of that one. Grace said her father brought it from Pennsylvania when he was courting Hannah."

Grace returned with plates of spaghetti, meatballs and sauce, and John jumped up to bring in the bread and butter. Everyone took their seats, they bowed their heads for a silent grace, Amish-style, and then they began to enjoy the delicious meal. It seemed that all three of them had had a good day. Grace had scored well on a test at the community college where she was studying to be a vet tech, and John had successfully delivered a litter of four healthy Cavalier King Charles Spaniels by caesarean section.

As they finished supper, Albert remembered the box of cookies he'd picked up at the German bakery. "Wait right here," he said. "I brought dessert. It won't take a moment to fetch it."

"We won't be able to walk away from the table," Grace teased.

"Then you can just roll me out of the house."

Albert got out of his chair. "But I'll bounce down the steps with a grin on my face."

"Uncle Albert, I'll get them." Grace put her hand on his shoulder as she passed him. "You sit. I forgot to pick up the mail, and I have to walk right past your truck. Come on, Blue," she called to the dog. "Want to take a walk?"

John refilled Albert's glass, Albert sat down again and John shared a joke Milly had told him. Albert laughed so hard he almost choked on his iced tea.

"You're in a good mood tonight," John said thoughtfully. "We've been worried about you since Gramps died. You really haven't seemed like yourself."

"It's not easy losing your father. He had his health problems, and I know he was right with his salvation. But I do miss him every day."

"I miss him, too," John agreed. "Without him— without the two of you—I wouldn't be where I am today. I'd never have gotten through school if—"

"Now, none of that," Albert said, his cheeks flushing with embarrassment. "You would have found your way." Still, John's admission warmed him inside. "You're right, though. I *have* been down in the dumps. Maybe some of it is realizing that when the older generation passes on, I'm suddenly at the top of the hill looking down."

John laughed. "You're what, Uncle Albert? Fifty-five? That's hardly over the hill."

"Fifty-six in July." Albert grimaced. "Sound like I'm eighty-five sometimes, don't I? I should be around Dakota more. Kids keep you young."

John leaned forward. "Have you ever thought about moving in with us? We could build a whole basement suite and even put in a minikitchen, if you don't want to eat with us regularly."

Albert laid his hand over John's. "I have thought about it. I really appreciate the offer, but you and Grace need time and space to build your own family."

John nodded. "You're sure?"

Albert nodded.

"Well, if you ever change your mind, the offer stands. We'd love to have you here, and it wouldn't hurt to have a built-in babysitter." They both laughed.

"I'll manage on my own just fine," Albert assured him.

"I know you will. I just worry. Maybe you need a hobby. Something to occupy your time when you're not working." John met Albert's gaze. "Because you can't just work, go to church and come here for dinner once a week. You need something more."

"Like what? Playing golf? Jet skiing?"

Again they laughed, because while many men his age might take up either, they weren't and never would be choices Albert would make.

Grace and Blue returned to the house, and then they enjoyed the cookies. It was eight forty-five when Albert drove away. As he turned onto the blacktop, he glanced back at the house. John was right. He had been happier tonight than he'd been since before Pop's health had taken a turn for the worse. It didn't pay for a man to brood on what he didn't have. Maybe John was right; maybe he needed a hobby. He needed something, but that something wasn't moving in with John's family.

He had his work: hard, stressful and challenging. He had friends, John, Grace and Dakota, as well as a great staff. He had his faith, so why did he feel that something was lacking in his life? Was it something—or someone? Maybe fifty-five wasn't over the hill. If he put his mind to it, maybe he could find a way to be happier every day.

He'd actually been thinking about taking up a hobby, of sorts. One of his elderly clients had been the one to plant the seed in his mind and had been generous enough to offer to help get him started. The idea definitely interested him. The thing was, he would need some help.

One person immediately came to mind.

But did he dare ask her?

* * *

Hannah let the school children out early on Friday. There were only a few full days left before the end-of-year picnic that marked the beginning of summer vacation. The English public schools ended in June, but Amish children were needed to help with spring planting. The Seven Poplars School began in September and closed at the end of April. Amish students had fewer vacation days during the year so that they could satisfy the state education requirements and still be finished early. For several of Hannah's students, this, their eighth year, would be their last. They would go on to learn a trade and begin their vocational training.

This should have been her foster son, Irwin's, final year of formal schooling, but she had yet to decide if he would be among the graduates. Irwin had never been a scholar. He'd come to her when he was twelve, already far behind his classmates, and each milestone in his education had been a hard-won goal. Hannah wasn't satisfied with Irwin's math skills or his reading comprehension, but she also worried that another year in the back of her classroom would make little difference. Irwin was tired of being shown up by younger students.

Hannah cared deeply about the orphaned boy. Although he had shown little natural ability at caring for animals or general farm work, Irwin had a good heart. She felt instinctively that he needed male guidance to help him develop the skills that would enable him to support himself and, someday, a family.

Hannah supposed that she'd done well enough for her daughters after her husband's passing, but she was beginning to wonder if she would have been wiser to remarry, as everyone had urged her. Few widows in their forties remained single after the customary year of mourning. Maybe she'd been selfish and a little proud to think that she could fill Jonas's shoes. What was the old saying? *A woman might be the heart of the family, but the man was the head.*

After the children had spilled out of the schoolhouse doors and run, walked or ridden their scooter push-bikes home, Hannah packed up to leave. There was plenty to do to prepare the school for the coming celebration, but the weather was so warm, the air so full of spring and the earth so green, Hannah couldn't bear to remain cooped up inside another moment. This was her favorite time of the year, when new life sprang from every inch of field and forest, a time when she felt that anything was possible.

Whistling a spritely tune, a habit for which she had been chastised many times as a child, Hannah walked down the dirt lane, across a clearing and climbed the stile that marked the boundary between her son-in-law Samuel's dairy farm and her own place. What would she do when she got home? Rebecca was at Miriam and Ruth's place and wouldn't be coming home for supper, and Irwin had gone off with his cousins, so it would be just her and Susanna.

When they'd parted after breakfast, Susanna had been unnaturally subdued, still unhappy about the punishment that Hannah had given her after the pizza escapade two days before. She'd forbidden Susanna from seeing David for an entire week.

Hannah had not, however, spoken to Susanna about her visit with David's mother. In fact, she hadn't spoken of it to anyone. Hannah couldn't imagine what Sadie was thinking bringing up the idea of Susanna and David marrying. It was, of course, not possible. David would never learn a trade or how to farm; Susanna was unable to run a household. They certainly couldn't be married.

Hannah pushed the whole idea from her mind, returning to thoughts of her pouting daughter. Susanna hadn't been happy about the forced separation between her and David, but Hannah was determined to be firm. She couldn't allow Susanna to do as she pleased. Her daughter's judgment had been poor, and she had to suffer the consequences. Still, Hannah wasn't angry with her, and she was determined to find something special and fun for the two of them to do together this afternoon.

"*Ne, Mam.* Going to Anna's." Susanna held up a book. "Naomi wants it." She moved to the nearest bookshelf and began to straighten the books. "I will eat supper with Anna. She said."

Hannah didn't know whether to be amused or feel rebuffed. Susanna's reply had been only mildly intoned, but her expression was a stubborn *"So there, Mam!"* It was clear to Hannah that her daughter was still out of sorts with her over the whole David King mishap and was determined to exert her independence. Somehow, in Susanna's mind, sneaking out of the house and the accident with the buggy had been Hannah's fault and not hers.

"I'm the li-bair-ian," Susanna said. "I can't stay here. Have to take the book to Naomi."

Hannah folded her arms. "I see." Clearly, what Grace had said recently was true. Susanna had always developed slower than her sisters, but at almost twenty-one, she had charged headlong into her own form of independence.

When Hannah had turned their unused milk house into a lending library for the local Amish community, she'd suggested that Susanna become the librarian. She'd hoped the responsibility would give Susanna a sense of self-worth. Despite her struggles with the written word, Susanna had taken to the job with great enthusiasm. She could read only a little, and Hannah suspected that much of Susanna's pleasure from the library came from arranging the books by color and requiring users to print their names and the borrowed titles in a large journal.

Susanna and the whole family enjoyed providing suitable books for their neighbors, adults and children alike. But what Hannah hadn't expected was that David King would become an almost daily visitor to Susanna's library, or that the two of them would spend so many hours in the small building laughing and talking together. Hannah was afraid that David was borrowing so many books as an excuse to see Susanna, something definitely against the rules for Amish young people of marriageable age. The trouble was, how did she put an end to an innocent friendship?

"You're walking across the field, aren't you?" Hannah asked, more as a reminder than a question. "You aren't walking down the road?"

"*Ya*. The pasture. I can do it by myself."

"Be home by seven. Ask one of the twins to walk back with you."

"By myself, *Mam*." Susanna threw her a look so much like her sister Johanna's that Hannah smiled.

"All right. By yourself, but be careful, Susanna. No talking to strangers."

Susanna giggled and folded her arms in a mirror image of Hannah. "No strangers in the pasture."

Hannah sighed. "No, I suppose there aren't. But be careful, just the same." Feeling a little out of sorts with herself, Hannah left the library and went back into the house. There, she looked around for something out of place or something that needed doing, but all seemed in order.

The house echoed with emptiness. Chores done, floors scrubbed, dishes washed and put away. Susanna had been busy today, so busy that she'd left nothing for Hannah to do. And with all her children active in their own families, Hannah knew she should have been glad for the peace and quiet. No grandchildren running through the house, no slamming doors, no tracking mud through the kitchen, no supper to cook.

Of course, she would need some sort of supper for herself. Maybe she'd start something that she, Susanna, Rebecca and Irwin could have again tomorrow. Hannah wanted to begin setting out early vegetable plants in the garden, and she wouldn't have time to prepare a big noon meal. She went to the refrigerator, but when she opened it, there was a pot of chicken and dumplings as well as a bowl of coleslaw. A note was propped in front. "Enjoy! Rice pudding on bottom shelf. Love, Johanna."

Hannah sighed. Why did Johanna's thoughtful

deed add to her sense of restlessness? Maybe she should walk over to Ruth's and see if she needed help with the twins. Or, perhaps she should check on the chickens to see if Susanna had remembered to gather the eggs. Taking a basket from a peg on the wall, Hannah went back into the yard.

She was halfway to the chicken house when she heard the sound of a motor vehicle. As she watched, a familiar truck came up the lane and into the yard. Albert pulled to a stop, rolled down the window and smiled.

"Afternoon, Hannah."

"Afternoon, Albert." She walked over to his truck, egg basket on her arm.

"Wondered how the pony was, if you noticed any swelling in his legs or any bruising?"

She shook her head. "*Ne*. The pony is fine, thanks be."

"And Susanna? She's no worse for the tumble?" He tugged at his ball cap and leaned out the window.

"*Ne*, Susanna's good." She chuckled. "Actually, she's not behaving like herself. She's always been the easiest of my children, but recently…" She spread her hands. "I know you don't have children, but…"

"No, I don't, but I think I should have. Sometimes, Hannah, I wonder if…"

"*Ya?*"

He removed his cap and squeezed the brim between his hands, then put it back on his head and tugged it tight. "You sure you don't want me to check that pony out?"

"The pony's fine." First Susanna and now Albert. This was turning into the strangest afternoon, Hannah mused. She liked the man, found his company interesting and felt at ease with him, but she couldn't imagine why he was acting so oddly.

It seemed almost as if Albert wanted to say something but couldn't bring himself to do it. He was like a father to Grace's husband. Was there some trouble with Grace's new family that she didn't know about? Hannah's eyes narrowed. And why was Albert so worried about Susanna? Was there more about Susanna and David than what he'd told her?

"If you've something to tell me," she said. "It's best you just say it instead of beating around the bush."

Albert's earnest face flushed.

Bingo, she thought. But she didn't urge him further. If there was one thing that she'd learned from being a teacher, it was that silence often brought more confessions than demands did.

"There is something I wanted to ask you."

"*Ya,* Albert. What is it?"

He leaned out the window. "Well, I've been doing a lot of thinking about…"

It was all she could do to keep from tapping her foot impatiently. "Yes, Albert?"

"Alpacas," he said.

# Chapter Four

Albert raised his gaze to meet Hannah's. He could feel his face growing warm. Being around Hannah Yoder always did that to him. Made him tongue-tied, too.

It wasn't just that Hannah was attractive. She was that and more. Maybe attractive didn't do her justice. Hannah was strikingly handsome, with large brown eyes, a generous mouth and a shapely nose with just a smattering of freckles. Hers wasn't a face a man was likely to forget, no matter his age.

Hannah's creamy skin was as smooth as a baby's, and her hair, what he could see of it, peeking out around her *kapp,* was thick and curly, a soft reddish-brown. She was tall, but not too tall, sturdy, but still graceful. He'd never seen her when she wasn't neat and tidy.

It wasn't just her looks that he liked. Hannah

was the sort of woman you expected could take charge if she needed to. Something about her was calming, which didn't make much sense, considering that she always put him off his stride when she was near him. But one thing was certain, she didn't look or act old enough to have grandbabies.

Not that he thought of her as anything but a friend. Their relationship was solidly defined by the rules of what it meant to be Amish and Mennonite. And the fact that they could both acknowledge their friendship and be easy with one another was a tribute to Hannah's respected status among both communities. And, he hoped, to his own.

"Albert?"

Hannah's voice slid through his thoughts like warm maple syrup. She had a way of pronouncing his name that gave it a German lilt, but seemed perfectly natural. He blinked. "Yes, Hannah?"

"Did you say *alpacas?*" Her eyes twinkled, as though she'd heard something amusing but was too kind to laugh at him.

*"Ya,"* he said, falling into the *Deitsch* speech pattern that his family had often used when he was a youngster on the farm. "You've heard of alpacas, haven't you?"

She chuckled. "I have. My friend in Wisconsin raises them. She cards the fleece after she shears it, spins it, and sells the fiber to English women who knit garments out of it. It's much warmer than sheep's wool, too warm for Delaware use. But it's very soft and she gets a good price for it."

"Well," He hesitated, not wanting her to think that he hadn't seriously considered what he was about to propose. "John thinks that I have too much time on my hands," he said. "Since my father…" He took a breath and started again, wondering if coming to Hannah with this scheme had been a big mistake. "The practice keeps me pretty busy, and of course, I'm always welcome at Grace and John's, but…"

She was just looking at him in that patient way of hers, and he finished in a rush. "John suggested, and I thought it was a good idea, for me to take up a hobby."

She nodded. "I can see where that would make sense, Albert."

Again, he noticed her unique way of saying his name. Hannah's English was flawless, but some words came out with just a hint of German accent.

"And you've been thinking about raising alpacas? Is that what you're saying?" She motioned toward the house. "I've got iced tea chilling in the refrigerator. It's warm this afternoon, and I'm sure you must be thirsty. Would you like some?"

"I would," he answered, getting out of the truck. "That's kind of you. If it's no trouble."

"How much trouble could pouring a glass of

tea be?" Hannah led the way toward a picnic table standing in the shade of a tree beside the house. "Have a seat, Albert." He did, and she went into the house through the back door and returned with two glasses of iced tea.

He nodded his thanks, accepted the glass and took a sip of the tea. It was delicious, not too sweet. "Great. Is that mint I taste?"

Hannah's eyes twinkled. "That's Susanna's doing. It does give the tea a refreshing bite, doesn't it?" Hannah sat down across the table from him. He nodded, and then drew the conversation back to his reason for stopping by today. "So I was saying, about the alpacas. As it happens, an acquaintance of mine, another vet over in Talbot County—that's in Maryland—"

Hannah chuckled. "I know where Talbot County is, Albert. Jonas and I bought cows from a farmer there regularly."

"That's right, I remember. Jonas told me that. Anyway, one of this vet's clients, an older man, has a herd of alpacas. Mr. Gephart has had some health problems and he needs to find homes for most of his stock. He's willing to sell me some of his *hembras*—that's what they call the females— at an excellent price if I promise to keep them together. Mr. Gephart has become very fond of them, and he's raised them from *crias*."

"*Crias* are the babies," Hannah said. "I remember my Wisconsin friend mentioning that. She said that they are really cute."

He leaned forward, pleased that Hannah seemed interested in hearing about the alpacas. "One of the females has a *cria*. It's a male, and he's all black. The mother is a rose-gray color, and her name is Estrella. She's gentle and her fleece is especially fine, but she had some problems when the baby was born. She won't be able to have any more little ones, but she's a dominant female, and she'd make an excellent leader for the herd. They live fifteen to twenty years, so she'd produce fleece for a long time. I'm thinking I won't get a male of my own, at least to start with."

"It sounds as if you've made up your mind to start your own herd," she said.

"Pretty much, but here's the thing." He took another swallow of the tea. He'd rehearsed what he would say to Hannah, how he would present his proposal, but his thoughts were all a jumble in his head now. "You know I have that property on Briar Corner Road?" he started slowly. "I've got about seventy acres there. Anyway, that would be a good place for the alpacas if I had fencing and a decent barn, but the place is sort of isolated. There would be no one to keep an eye on them."

"I see your point," she agreed. "Alpacas are a big investment, and without someone living there, you couldn't be sure that your animals would be safe."

"They're just like any other livestock. They're best kept close. So, what I was wondering is…" He took another drink of tea. "You have this empty second barn and a lot of outbuildings, and you've got first-class fencing. I was hoping that you might consider boarding my alpacas. They wouldn't need much room, five acres at most. And I wouldn't expect you to do the feeding and care. I could come by morning and evening and—"

"Albert." Hannah tilted her head and fixed him with her schoolteacher stare.

"I'm sure we could agree on a fair monthly price. I'd feel so much better about starting the venture if my animals were here." Now that he was on a roll, he just kept going. "Your little stable would make a perfect—"

"Please, stop." She raised a hand, palm up.

He broke off in midsentence, and his expression must have shown his disappointment because she hurried to go on.

"I'm not saying no. What I'm saying is …" She shrugged. "How many times have we had you or John here in the past year to help one of our animals?"

"Not counting the pony?" He paused to consider. "Six, seven times, maybe."

"A lot more than that." She smiled at him.

"You've been more than fair with billing us, but still having the proper veterinary care for animals is a big part of our expense." She settled back on the bench and folded her arms. "Why don't we strike a bargain? I'll provide housing and grazing for your alpacas, and you do my veterinary care free of charge for six months? Then we can decide if we want to continue with the arrangement as it is, or make changes."

Relief surged through him. After thinking on the whole idea for a few days, he was really keen on it. It excited him in a way nothing had in a good long while. Mr. Gephart wanted to downsize his herd as soon as possible, and a delay might mean Albert would lose the opportunity. "You'll do it? Without being paid? That hardly seems fair to you—"

She chuckled. "I think I'm in a better place to decide what's fair to me. I like the idea of having animals in those empty stalls. And I have a lot of livestock that need vet care: the pigs, cows, horses. Not to mention the cats people keep dropping off here. Having them neutered or spayed is a drain on my pocketbook, but if I don't have it done, I'd end up buried in hundreds of cats."

He nodded. "I can see your point." Straightening his shoulders, he took another drink of the tea. "I'm thinking of buying seven alpacas to start. Three of the *hembras* are pregnant, and the other females are nearly old enough to—" The word *breed* stuck in his throat and he felt his throat clench.

"It's all right, Albert," Hannah assured him with a sweet, mischievous smile. "I'm a farmer. I understand the process. Unless you're raising the alpacas just as a hobby, you'll want young ones to add to your herd and to sell to help cover expenses."

"Exactly." He drained the last of his tea. "Is it all right if I walk back and take a look at the stable, to see what I'd need to do to bring the animals home?"

"Of course. I'll come with you." Hannah rose and they walked side by side across the yard toward the second, smaller barn and the outbuildings. "There's a small attached pound, a loafing shed and a seven-acre pasture with good grazing, beyond that. As you can see, this field is far back, away from the road."

"It looks perfect."

"I'm fortunate. My son-in-law Charley believes in good fences. I don't know what I'd do without him doing the heavy work on the farm."

"Miriam picked a good husband," Albert agreed. Neither of them mentioned that his nephew, John, had seriously courted Hannah's daughter Miriam, before she'd accepted Charley's offer of marriage. John had been hurt and disappointed at losing Miriam, but that was before he'd met Grace. Now both couples were happily married, and Hannah had the satisfaction of knowing that her Miriam would remain securely in the Amish faith.

"There's no reason for you to stop by every morning," Hannah said as she unlatched the door to the stable. "Our windmill pumps fresh water into the stable and to the trough in the loafing shed. One of us can easily do the first feeding when we tend the other animals. I know that mornings are your busiest time of the day."

"They are," he agreed. "But I wouldn't want to put you out. You're doing me a big favor by letting me keep them here."

"There'll be no talk of favors," she said, smiling so hard that a dimple appeared on her cheek. "We're just old friends, helping each other out."

Hannah showed him the empty small barn with the spacious box stalls, the feed storage area and the door that led into the pound or corral, as horse people liked to refer to it. The stable was as clean as he'd expected. Alpacas were herd animals so they wouldn't really need individual stalls, but he was glad to see that there were two separate wooden enclosed areas where an injured animal or an expectant female could be cared for. A narrow staircase against one wall led to a half loft overhead.

She pushed open the wide back door. It was built in the old Dutch manner, split, so that the top half could be swung open with the bottom remaining fastened. "You can see what the fence is like from here," she explained.

As he'd expected, Hannah's wooden posts were solid, the stock wire was tight, and the open loafing shed dry and clean. He couldn't have designed anything better for the alpacas if he'd had the time to build out at his farm. Hannah's place was also closer and more convenient to get to. He was sure this would work out fine. "I'll not be a bother to you," he promised.

"I know you won't. But I warn you, you may have to chase off my grandchildren. I think your alpacas are going to be a big hit with them."

"The animals are gentle and sweet-natured," he assured her. "I think that you'll be a fan, too."

As they were leaving the barn, Albert heard the rattle of buggy wheels on the driveway and saw a horse pulling a two-wheel cart coming up the driveway. An Amish woman was driving the open carriage.

Hannah raised her hand to shade her eyes from the late afternoon sun. "Why, that looks like Aunt Jezzy!" she exclaimed. "What a nice surprise."

"I'll be getting back to the office," Albert said. He was a little disappointed. He'd been hoping to talk with Hannah a little longer. He had a lot of questions to ask, like if Hannah had straw for bedding to sell, or if she thought he'd be better off ordering woodchips for the stalls. "I don't want to interfere with your company."

"You'll do no such thing," Hannah said. "Wait right here for a moment until I see if Aunt Jezzy has come on an errand or has time to visit. Don't move an inch, Albert." She hurried over to meet the older woman who'd, until not long ago, had been part of her household. Aunt Jezzy had recently married and lived not far from Byler's Store. Today, she didn't have her husband with her; she was alone in the cart.

Hannah greeted her aunt and the two exchanged hugs. They were talking, but they were too far away for Albert to make out what they were saying. Then Hannah turned back and motioned to him. "Aunt Jezzy's come to spend the night with me," she called. "And we'd love it if you'd stay and share supper with us. I've got chicken and dumplings."

Albert's first thought was to refuse. He glanced at his watch. They closed the clinic early on Fridays, and he hadn't had any emergency calls. But surely Hannah was just being polite; she didn't really want him to stay. He couldn't remember anything particular in the refrigerator, but he could always stop and pick up a frozen pizza on the way back to his apartment. "Thanks," he said. "It's kind of you, but I—"

"Homemade coleslaw, some of Anna's yeast rolls and rice pudding with raisins for dessert," Hannah tempted. "Come on, Albert. I know you love chicken and dumplings."

He did. Next to chicken and dumplings, another frozen pizza sounded about as good as a Frisbee with a little ketchup drizzled on it. "You're sure I won't be a bother?" He walked toward them. "I really should…"

"Accept our invitation," Hannah urged. "I know Aunt Jezzy would love to hear about your alpacas."

Albert considered the situation. Jezzy's visit was his good luck. As accepting as the Amish were of him, they had their rules. One was that he couldn't be in a house alone with a woman or a girl of any age. He hadn't seen Susanna or Rebecca around, but having Hannah's aunt present made it perfectly acceptable for him to join them for the evening meal.

"All right," he said, giving in graciously. "I never could pass up a home-cooked meal that I didn't cook." He chuckled. "And I'd walk a mile in bare feet for homemade rice pudding."

Hannah smiled as Albert finished off a second helping of chicken and dumplings. It was always good to have company, and having Aunt Jezzy come by when she did was a delight. It was nice to see a man eat heartily at her table. Hannah guessed that Albert made do for himself with fast food and sandwiches more than he should. At least that's what Grace had shared when she was visiting a few days earlier.

*John and I worry about Uncle Albert,* Grace had said. *Since John's grandfather passed away, Uncle Albert's all alone in that apartment over the office. He never was much of a cook, according to John, and we're concerned for his health. Sometimes, John says he makes do with bologna-and-cheese sandwiches or just peanut butter and crackers for supper. And he starts work with coffee and a donut.*

Albert's a man who enjoys plain country cooking when it's put in front of him, Hannah thought. She'd believed that Grace's husband, John, had the biggest appetite she'd seen on a normal-size man, but now she knew where John had gotten it. Albert was so polite that he was almost shy. He had to be coaxed to take a decent portion, then seconds, but it was clear he savored every bite. Even Aunt Jezzy took pleasure in watching him enjoy his food.

Aunt Jezzy's husband had gone to visit a dying cousin in Lancaster. She never liked being alone in a house, so she'd hitched up the buggy and

come for an overnight visit. Naturally, since neither of them had a telephone in the house, there
was no way Aunt Jezzy could let her know she
was coming, but she'd been certain of her welcome here.

This afternoon Hannah had been feeling lonely
and out of sorts. Then Albert had showed up with
his plan for the alpacas, brightening her day.
There was no way she could have invited Albert
to share her evening meal without anyone else
present. It simply wouldn't have been proper. A
good Amish woman did not entertain a man without a chaperone.

Then here was Aunt Jezzy, a gift from God, as
it were, making it possible for Hannah to invite
them both to share the food that her thoughtful
daughter had left for her. It just went to prove that
the Lord's mercy was unending. She had been
feeling sorry for herself, wallowing in self-pity
because she had to eat alone, and He had wiped
away her gloom in an instant with an unexpected
gift of sunshine.

Hannah glanced across the table with a smile.
She could see that Albert was enjoying himself as
much as she was. With a little urging, he began to
explain his plan for raising alpacas; her aunt was
fascinated. Aunt Jezzy had always loved animals.
Actually, Hannah couldn't think of anything or
anyone her aunt-by-marriage didn't like.

Some people thought Jezzy was odd, and she did have some curious habits, such as spinning spoons and turning objects around three times before she could let them rest. But Albert never seemed to notice Aunt Jezzy's endearing little quirks. The three of them weren't halfway through supper when Albert had them laughing so hard with tales from his veterinary practice that she almost dropped her glass.

Not that Albert mentioned any names or repeated anything he shouldn't, but surely it couldn't be a sin to be amused by stories of a man who let his pet pig sleep in a bed in his house and tied a ribbon around its head.

"As I live and breathe," Aunt Jezzy said, wiping her eyes with her napkin. "How could anybody be that silly?"

Chuckling, Hannah rose and went to the refrigerator for the rice pudding. "Are you sure you won't have more coleslaw?" she asked Albert. "And there's more chicken and dumplings in the pot."

"Not another mouthful," Albert protested. "I'll never make it up the stairs to my apartment. I can't tell you how much I've enjoyed myself, being with you two, and sharing your supper. I really appreciate it."

"*Ne, ne,* none of that," Hannah said. "It was our pleasure." The mantel clock chimed, and she glanced up. Was it truly that late? She glanced out the windows to see if she could catch sight of either of her daughters. Of course, it was Susanna she was most concerned about. Rebecca was so busy with wedding plans that she often stayed at one of her sisters' houses until well after dark.

A small concern nagged at Hannah as she served up generous bowls of the rice pudding. "Would anyone like coffee?" She wondered if it would be an imposition to ask Albert to drive by Anna's and tell Susanna to start for home, if her daughter didn't get home before he left, that was.

But, there was no need. They'd barely started their pudding when the dogs outside began to bark, and Samuel's buggy came into the yard.

Hannah went out onto the back porch. To her surprise, it wasn't Samuel but her daughter Anna who, along with Susanna, was getting down from the buggy. Before Hannah reached the back gate, Susanna handed Anna's little daughter, Rose, down to Anna.

*"Mam!"* Anna waved. "I hope you don't mind, but I've come to spend the night. I just thought I'd use the excuse of driving Susanna home to take a little vacation."

"Wonderful," Hannah said, smiling back at her. She was always pleased to see Anna. Her daughter's round, pink cheeks glowed with health, and she looked as jolly as ever. Of all her children,

Anna and Susanna had always been the easiest to raise.

"Samuel can mind the children tonight," Anna declared. "Baby Rose and I thought it might be fun to surprise you."

*"Ya."* Susanna giggled. "A surprise for you, *Mam.* I brought Anna and Rose. To sleep with us."

"Wonderful," Hannah said, taking the baby from Anna's arms. "Aunt Jezzy is here to stay the night, too. We'll have our own frolic."

Anna got a bag with their things from the back of the buggy and placed it on the ground. "I'll just unhitch the horse and put him in the barn." She glanced at Albert's truck. "None of your animals are sick, are they?"

*"Ne,* all are fine. Aunt Jezzy and I asked Albert to share supper with us. Grace says he never takes time for a proper meal."

"Good of you, *Mam,* to invite him."

Hannah nuzzled the sweet softness of Rose's neck. "I can't wait to tell you my news." She shifted the baby to her hip. Rose laughed and snatched at Hannah's *kapp* ribbon.

Anna's hearty chuckle echoed through the farmyard. "I warn you. She's teething. Anything she can fit in her mouth, she will. She'll eat your *kapp* if you let her."

Hannah smiled and bounced Rose, and the baby giggled. Could this day get any better? "Albert wants to buy a herd of alpacas, and he's going to keep them here," she told Anna. "We've made a trade. My empty stalls and pasture for his veterinary care."

"Sounds like a good deal to me," Anna said.

"Al-pack-ers?" Susanna asked.

"Alpacas. You'll see." Hannah slipped her free arm around Susanna and hugged her. "I was starting to wonder if you would be home before dark."

"I told you," Susanna said with a determined nod. "I am re-pon-sible."

"Sometimes," Anna teased.

*"Ya,"* Susanna echoed. "Sometimes."

"I'll just be a few minutes," Anna called as she led the horse and buggy away. "And I have news for you, too, *Mam.*"

"Good news I hope?" She didn't want to hear bad news, not tonight, not when everything was going so well.

"Good," Susanna said. "Samuel is building Rose a big girl bed."

Anna shrugged and grinned. *"Ya,* she's right, *Mam.* I think the Lord will send us a new little one to sleep in Rose's cradle before Christmas."

"Truly?" Hannah asked. "You and Samuel are blessed with another child?"

"We are," Anna replied. "And this one feels different." She grinned. "I told Samuel maybe this one will be another little wood chopper."

## Chapter Five

With all the women in the house, Hannah fully expected Albert to finish his rice pudding and make his escape, but—surprising her once again—he didn't. And in the hour between Anna and Susanna's arrival and Albert's departure, he told the two of them all about his alpacas, showed everyone pictures of them on his cell phone and bounced Rose on his knee when she became fussy. He even produced a ball of alpaca fleece from his jeans pocket so Susanna could feel how soft it was.

"Albert is nice," Susanna said when his truck pulled out of the yard at seven-thirty. "I'm going to give King David my wool." She held up the fluffy alpaca ball for her mother to see. "Albert said it was mine."

"Of course, you can give it to David, if you want. But maybe you should keep it. Wouldn't it be fun to learn to spin the fleece into yarn?" Hannah was pleased that the Susanna who'd returned with Anna wasn't the sullen girl who, earlier in the day, had strode off across the pasture pouting. Hannah was concerned that David was still on her mind. But, at least this evening, she had her sweet, easygoing daughter back.

"Albert is English, but nice," Susanna declared, scraping her pudding bowl to get the last spoonful of dessert.

*"Ne,"* Anna corrected with a smile. "Albert is a Mennonite like Grace and John. Not Plain, but not English, either."

"And 'Kota." Susanna licked the back of her spoon. "Can I have more?"

Hannah shook her head. "One bowl of rice pudding is plenty. You can have more for breakfast, if you like." Susanna had had supper at Anna and Samuel's table, and Hannah guessed that her daughter had already eaten enough. Like 'Kota and her other young nieces and nephews, Susanna had trouble knowing when to stop eating sweets.

Rose, who'd been toddling around the kitchen, plopped onto her bottom and gave a little wail. Anna put out her arms. "Come here, my dumpling."

"Let me." Aunt Jezzy picked up the baby and settled into the rocking chair with her. Rose fussed for a few moments, and then gave in to the steady movement and the gentle patting on her back and fell asleep. "This one is easily soothed," the older woman pronounced.

Hannah glanced at her granddaughter and smiled. "Like Anna," she said. "You were always a contented baby, Anna."

"Let's hope this next one will be the same," Anna said. "Not like those two boys of mine. I have to keep them busy, else—" She arched her eyebrows and shook her head.

Hannah pulled off her shoes and put them beside Susanna's by the kitchen door. Hearing Anna speak of the twins like that made her feel warm and happy inside. When Samuel, their neighbor, had married Anna, a woman much younger than he was, he'd brought five children to the union. Rose was their first baby together, but to hear Anna tell it, she was the mother of all six. It was a fine match and Samuel obviously loved and adored Anna, despite her plumpness.

Deep in thought, Hannah poured herself a cup of mint tea and sat down at the table across from Anna and Susanna. God's plan for Anna had been the perfect one for her, she thought. He'd truly blessed her with a home and family. But now that all of her daughters but one would soon be settled, Hannah could only hope and pray that He would remember to keep His eye on her special child.

"Why don't we go out onto the front porch,

*Mam,*" Anna suggested. "It's so warm this evening. And I think it's too early in the year for mosquitoes."

*"Ya,"* Hannah agreed as she stirred sugar into her tea. "There's a nice breeze out there." She reached out to pat Susanna's small hand. "Don't you want to shower and wash your hair?"

Susanna shook her head. "Don't want to go to bed. Want to sit on the front porch with you and Anna and Aunt Jezzy."

"Did I say anything about going to bed?" Hannah asked. "It's early yet. But wouldn't you feel comfy in your nightgown and slippers?"

Susanna grinned broadly, then giggled. "Outside? In my nightgown?"

Anna chuckled. "Why not? There's no one here but us girls tonight. It sounds nice. Maybe I'll put mine on, too."

Susanna's slanting, blue eyes narrowed with suspicion. "Not sleepy."

Anna chuckled and slipped an arm around her sister. "You heard *Mam,* Susanna-Banana. You don't have to go to sleep. But I'm going to wash my hair. If you want, I'll help you wash yours."

"We can have a hair-braiding frolic," Aunt Jezzy suggested. "This little one is fast asleep. Shall I just tuck her into the crib in Hannah's room?"

*"Ya,* if you wouldn't mind," Anna said. "It's

what I love about coming home. Plenty of willing hands to take turns holding Rose. And now with the new one coming—"

"New one?" Aunt Jezzy's eyebrows shot up and her crooked smile widened. "I thought you looked particularly glowy, girl." She gently slid Rose's cap off her head and kissed the auburn curls. "I always thought I'd have a baby of my own," she murmured, more to herself than to the others. "But God has taken pity on me and blessed me in my old age with so many great-nieces and great-nephews to love."

Hannah's throat constricted as she thought of how long Aunt Jezzy had lived in the corners of her family's life, first her mother's, then her sister Lovina's and finally here. People had thought her odd, but her new husband didn't care. Who would have ever thought that after so many years a spinster, Aunt Jezzy would take a husband and flourish in her new life as mistress of her own home?

"Can we have popcorn?" Susanna asked.

Anna glanced at her mother, silently asking for permission, and when Hannah nodded, she assured Susanna that she could—as soon as she was showered. Mollified, Susanna agreed, and the two went off together.

Aunt Jezzy put Rose to bed, and Hannah made a large batch of buttered popcorn. When the girls came back downstairs with wet hair, hairbrushes,

combs and bobby pins, Hannah and Aunt Jezzy
were already seated on the porch with two large
bowls of popcorn and a pitcher of homemade root
beer. Both Hannah and her aunt had showered in
the downstairs bathroom, put on their own night-
gowns and had their wet hair wrapped in towels.

On the porch there was a swing and several
rockers, giving the occupants a fine view of the
farm. A line of trees across the front of the garden and the distance the house set back from the
road made the sitting area private. When Jonas
had been alive, they'd often taken their supper
on the porch, then relaxed there as the children
played on the lawn until bedtime. Hannah loved
to sit here in the evenings with the sound of crick-
ets and tree frogs and children's laughter. There
was something so peaceful about it, almost like
sitting in church and hearing the familiar words
of an old hymn.

"Is this a frolic?" Susanna asked as she helped
herself to a handful of buttered kernels. "A popcorn frolic?"

"A hair-braiding frolic," Anna said, choosing
the wide porch swing. She took the towel off her
head and shook out her long strawberry-blond
hair, running her fingers through it to make it
dry faster.

Motherhood had done little to whittle away
Anna's substantial size, Hannah mused. But Aunt

Jezzy was right: Anna did glow. She would never have the delicate features or the trim waists of her sisters, but Anna's inner beauty more than made up for it. "What does Samuel think of your coming child?" Hannah asked. "Is he happy?"

Crimson tinted Anna's plump cheeks. "He thanks God," she said. "We have prayed for another baby."

"I suppose he wants a boy," Aunt Jezzy said. She'd claimed the old green rocker next to Hannah, and motioned Susanna to come sit at her feet. "I'll braid your hair," she offered.

Susanna sat and drew her knees up. The long white nightdress, which belonged to one of her sisters once, more than covered her. Susanna was short, so that it hung below her ankles and dragged behind her when she walked. Hannah had offered to hem it, but Susanna wouldn't hear of it. The sleeping gown was cream-colored flannel, soft to the touch, and although it had no decoration, Susanna loved it so much that she often hid it so that Hannah wouldn't put it in the wash.

The previous afternoon, Hannah had found the garment rolled into a ball and tucked behind a stack of hymnbooks on the attic stairs. Apparently, Susanna had hidden it there several weeks ago and forgotten where she'd put it. She'd been certain that her mother had thrown the nightgown away, and when Hannah had taken it down off the wash line, clean and fresh, and carried it into the house in a basket of laundry, Susanna had been so happy that she'd snatched the gown up and hugged it to her.

*My dear little girl. How could David's mother ever think you could be a man's wife? Or think her son could be a husband?* David was able to read, but he didn't speak as well as Susanna. It was difficult for Hannah to know if he was more or less capable of caring for himself than Susanna was. David was a sweet boy, certainly. But no one would think of allowing two childlike adults to wed, and that was what Susanna and David were, what they would always be.

"Where are your elastics?" Aunt Jezzy asked Susanna. She glanced at Anna. "Did either of you bring down the rubber bands?"

Susanna giggled and clapped a small hand over her mouth in mock horror. "Forgot. Anna said, 'Susanna-Banana, get the hair ties.' But…" Susanna grimaced. "Forgot."

"Everyone forgets," Aunt Jezzy said. "One day I forgot it was visiting Sunday and got dressed for church."

Susanna giggled again.

"Could you go and get the elastics?" Anna asked. With a nod, Susanna got to her feet and hurried off. Anna glanced at her mother, once her sister was gone. "*Mam,* Susanna said something earlier tonight that troubles me. I don't like the idea of tattling on my little sister, but I think you should know. Susanna told Samuel at the supper table that she and David were courting."

Hannah rolled her eyes. "I know. I don't know how to convince her that it's not true. I keep telling her that she and David are just friends. That she can't court anyone. That I need her here with me, but I don't think she understands."

"She was also talking about getting married." Anna's tone was solemn.

"Well, you told her she wasn't, didn't you?"

"I didn't say anything. I just let it go." Anna pressed her lips together. "I wanted to talk to you to know how you wanted us to handle it."

"You don't see her," Aunt Jezzy mused aloud. "You look, Hannah, but…" She shook her head.

Hannah glanced at Jezzy. "What do you mean?"

"*Atch,* Hannah." She held up a finger, and for a moment an expression as shrewd as that of any of her sister Lovina's played over her soft face. "You do not see that your Susanna has grown into a young woman. You treat her like a child."

"She *is* a child," Hannah protested softly. "She'll always be—"

"*Ne, Mam,*" Anna said gently. "Susanna is no longer a child. She may not be quick about some things, but she feels as deeply as anyone, and whether you like the idea or not, she's convinced she has feelings for David. I think we need to be aware of those feelings and act accordingly."

A cold flood of guilt washed over Hannah as she realized the truth of Anna and Jezzy's words. As she recognized her own denial. If Jonas were here, he'd be so disappointed with her. She glanced from one of them to the other, and her distress must have shown because Anna patted the swing seat beside her.

"Come, sit here, *Mam*."

Hannah stood, crossed the porch to Anna's side, and sank onto the swing. "If you both thought I wasn't handling the situation with Susanna and David properly, why didn't you or your sisters say something to me earlier?"

Aunt Jezzy passed the hairbrush from hand to hand. "Little lambs will play. You must build tight fences," she murmured.

Hannah looked into Anna's beautiful eyes and read the compassion and love in them. "I have tried to do what's best for Susanna. You know I have."

"This isn't about blame, *Mam*. We're just saying that things have changed. That Susanna is…"

"Growing up." Hannah sighed.

"Yes," Anna agreed, patting her mother's hand. "Which means Susanna should have to follow the same rules about boys like every other girl her age in this community. The same rules we had to follow. We weren't allowed to spend time alone with boys, unchaperoned, and I don't think Susanna should be allowed to, either."

Hannah let Anna's words sink in. What Anna was suggesting was that she was giving Susanna too much freedom. She needed to keep a better eye on her youngest. A tighter rein. And she was probably right. Susanna was quick to move from one interest to the next. One week she would be trying to crochet dishcloths, the next, she would set aside her crochet needle to collect field flowers to dry in books. If Susanna spent less time with David, surely all this would die down. Of course that would mean Hannah would have to give up some of her own freedom. The truth was, she had gotten quite used to coming and going as she pleased more often as her daughters had left the fold one by one. Susanna had begun to show enough maturity to be left home alone and Hannah had allowed it. It was during those hours alone that she suspected Susanna was spending too much unsupervised time with David.

Hannah thought about the conversation she'd had with Albert before he'd left. He'd asked her if she wanted to ride down to the alpaca farm the following day with him. He was eager to tell Mr. Gephart that he'd made arrangements for stabling and that he wanted to finalize the sale. She'd agreed, but now she wondered if it was a good idea. She wouldn't feel comfortable leaving Susanna at home as she usually did, and Albert hadn't included her daughter in the invitation. Maybe it hadn't been wise to say she'd go anyway. Technically, she was a single woman and Albert was a single man. If she was going to hold Susanna to a higher standard, didn't she need to do the same for herself? She hated to go back on her word, but she'd have to tell Albert that she couldn't go when he stopped by for her after lunch.

Susanna's voice drifted through the open front door. She was singing a song, one that boys and girls favored at frolics. She was off-key, as usual, but Hannah had always found that endearing. Even now, Susanna's squeaky little voice triggered emotion in her, bringing a tightness to her chest. "I suppose it's time Susanna and I had a mother-daughter talk," she mused aloud. "But it wouldn't fare to confront her in front of you tonight. I wouldn't want her to think we're ganging up on her." She exhaled. "I'll speak to her about this in the morning."

After breakfast, Hannah followed Susanna outside to tend the chickens. From the barn, she could hear Irwin rattling the lid of the feed bin and calling to the cows. One of his cousins had come home with him and was helping with the chores. Here in the chicken house, there was some privacy.

The hens clucked and milled around, scratching at the kitchen scraps that Susanna tossed to them and snapping up the choice bits. Susanna loved the chickens. Often, Hannah would come out to find Susanna squatting on the ground outside, hugging a hen. She would lay her cheek against the sleek feathers, close her eyes and hum with contentment. The chickens, even the ill-tempered ones, would never peck Susanna.

Large windows filled one wall of the chicken house, making it bright inside. As always, it was clean and smelled of fresh straw. Jonas had believed that animals, even chickens, should live as clean as possible. "Clean water, good food and decent bedding is the best medicine for livestock and poultry," he would say. Hannah had believed him, and she'd never lowered the standards that he'd set.

"Susanna, we have to talk," she said softly. "About something you said yesterday. To Samuel and Anna." Susanna didn't respond, but that didn't mean she wasn't listening. "Did you tell Samuel that you and David were courting?"

"Yes-ter-day?" Susanna nibbled at her lower lip and suddenly became fascinated with a spot of sunshine on the sawdust-covered floor. "King David and me?"

No matter how many times Hannah explained that the young man's name was David King, not King David, Susanna continued to say it her way. And David's habit of wearing a paper crown from Burger King on his head didn't help.

"Susanna. You and David cannot court because you can't get married."

Susanna tilted her head and peered up slyly. "He said."

"Who said?"

"David. He said. He's going to get married." She pointed at herself. "To me."

"I'm sorry, Susanna, but David is wrong."

The door to the chicken house opened and Irwin stuck his head in. "Vernon had to go home. Do I have to clean the chicken house today? Did it last weekend."

*"Ya,"* Hannah said. "Every week, Irwin."

Susanna seized the opportunity to escape. While Hannah was giving Irwin directions, her daughter grabbed the scrap bucket and scooted out the door.

It was a little after one when Albert Hartman drove into the yard. Hannah, Irwin, Rebecca, Aunt Jezzy and Susanna had just finished the noon meal. Rebecca and Hannah had been going over arrangements for Rebecca's upcoming wedding to the new preacher, Caleb Wittner. The banns had already been called twice, and the service would be in May. Usually, weddings were planned for November, after the crops were in, but Caleb was a widower with a young child. Everyone was so pleased that he and Rebecca had chosen each other that people were willing to take a day off from the busy spring planting to witness the ceremony.

Albert pulled his big truck up near the gate closest to the kitchen. Hannah went out, followed closely by Irwin and Susanna. "There's no need for you two to come out," Hannah called over her shoulder. But they didn't return to the house. Instead, they stood on the porch steps and stared as if Albert hadn't driven into their yards dozens of times in the past.

Hannah was slightly piqued. It was a toss-up as to which of them, Irwin or Susanna, was the nosiest. She waved at Albert, sorry that she would have to tell him she couldn't go. Having to refuse his invitation at this point was something of an embarrassment. But she knew she had to do what was right for her family. As she started to walk toward the truck, her grandson 'Kota appeared in the open window in the backseat.

"Are you coming, *Mam?*" he asked excitedly. "I can't wait to see the baby alpaca."

Hannah's heart melted. Grace's son was technically a step-grandchild, but Hannah didn't see it that way. She loved him as much as she did Anna's Rose or Johanna's three, not to mention Ruth's twin boys. "*Mam* can't go," she said. "I've got too much work to do."

"But Mama said you…" His face crinkled with disappointment. "Mama said I could go because you were going."

For an instant, Hannah thought he would burst into tears. Strictly speaking, *Mam* was the name for mother, not grandmother, but 'Kota had copied Grace, and now he called her *Mam,* as her children did.

Albert, who'd gotten out of the truck, glanced at the boy and then back to Hannah. "What did you tell me, Hannah? That I work too hard? Well, the same can be said for you. Come on, go with us. I'm sure Susanna would like to come, as well."

"*Ya,*" Susanna called from the porch. "I want to come."

"Me, too," Irwin chimed in, hands thrust in his pockets. "Can I come?"

"Irwin," Hannah chided. "It isn't polite to invite yourself."

"The more the merrier," Albert insisted. "And it won't take all afternoon. We'll just head over, give the youngsters a chance to see the alpacas and come on home. What do you say, Hannah?"

What could she say? With 'Kota, Susanna and Irwin all staring at her with pleading eyes, she could hardly refuse. "All right," she agreed, good-naturedly. "Let me get my *kapp*. You, too, Susanna. Your good *kapp* and a clean apron."

Minutes later, they were all in Albert's large cab pickup truck, heading west toward Maryland and the alpaca farm.

# Chapter Six

"*Mam,* do you want me to start putting the salads into the buggy?" Rebecca asked. "I've put the ice in the coolers."

It was four o'clock on Wednesday afternoon, the day of the school picnic that signaled the end of the school year for Seven Poplars. Tuesday had been the end of classes, but this combined fundraiser and recognition day was one that parents, students and Hannah always eagerly looked forward to.

"Yes, thank you." Hannah said. "And the pies, too."

Hannah, Johanna, Rebecca and Susanna had been cooking and preparing dishes since early morning. And Hannah was certain that Anna's house had been a hum of activity, as well. Daughters Ruth and Miriam didn't have children in the school, but they'd gone over to help Anna after lunch. Irwin had already been dispatched to assist Miriam's husband, Charley, and Ruth's husband, Eli, in setting up the games and setting out tables for the picnic baskets.

"All done!" Susanna pronounced. A row of misshapen, crumbling whoopie pies lined the kitchen counter. Marshmallow cream filling oozed from between oversize chocolate cookies and dribbled down the cabinet doors to pool on the floor. Susanna's hands and mouth were gooey with marshmallow filling, but she was grinning from ear to ear. "Look, *Mam!*" she urged. "Look at my whoopie pies!"

Johanna and Rebecca exchanged looks, and Rebecca covered her mouth with her hand and coughed to suppress a giggle.

*"Gut."* Johanna handed her little sister a roll of wax paper. "Do you want me to help you wrap them?"

Susanna shook her head. *"Ne.* I can do it by myself." One by one, she laboriously tore off sheets of wax paper and swaddled the whoopie pies. The results were haphazard, to say the least, but Hannah only smiled and watched as Susanna added several of the sweets to her picnic basket and set the others aside to donate.

The picnic basket auction wouldn't be the only method of raising money that day. Donated pies, cakes and other baked goods were for sale as well as useful items such as buggy wheels, milk buckets, quilts, kitchenware and butter churns. Every penny raised would be put to good use at the school, but the parceling out of choice supper baskets was the prime entertainment of the event. Successes and failures of meals would be talked about for months, perhaps even years, and more than one courtship had started with a heavily laden basket of good food.

Every unmarried woman over the age of sixteen was expected to bring a meal that would be sold to the highest bidder. The custom was that any man could bid, and whoever succeeded in buying the basket would eat supper with the cook. This year, Hannah was preparing a supper basket. Not that she was looking for a beau. She'd not met anyone in the county who she could imagine exchanging vows with, but it seemed only fair that she do her share to support the fund-raiser as the other widows did.

None of the baskets were labeled, and there was always a great deal of nosing around so that eligible men could discover, prior to the auction, who had made which basket. When a bidder guessed wrong, the onlookers found it hilarious to see a young bachelor having to share supper with someone old enough to be his grandmother, while the girl he had his eye on spent time with someone else. But it was always all in good fun. Frolics were a time for the community to come together and relax, to share news and renew the ties to friends and family.

Hannah had intended to pack her meal in a big egg basket, but the previous night, her mother-in-law, Lovina, had insisted on taking the basket home to use herself. The elderly woman, who made her home with Anna and Samuel, had periods of memory loss and what the Englishers called dementia. Lovina often believed that her son Jonas, Hannah's late husband, was still alive. Sometimes, she mistook Samuel for Jonas, a notion Samuel was too kindhearted to dispute. In any case, Lovina, who was having a good week, had insisted that she, too, was going to bring a basket supper to the school frolic, but wanted her daughter-in-law's basket. Hannah didn't mind, not even when Lovina sent over an ancient lidded wicker basket, tied shut with yarn, for Hannah to use.

The basket Hannah had packed, with its lid tied shut, obviously belonged to an elderly woman. There was little chance anyone would be eager to bid on it, but Samuel had already offered to buy it so Hannah would get to share the evening meal with Anna and her family. As for Lovina, she just might get to enjoy someone else's company, and would be glowing like newly churned butter.

"Ready," Susanna declared, lugging her basket toward the kitchen door.

The sound of glass jars clinking caused Hannah to raise an eyebrow. "What did you pack in there besides your whoopie pies?"

"Pickles and peanut butter."

"Peanut-butter-and-pickle sandwiches?" Rebecca asked.

Susanna shook her head. "Jar of peanut butter. Jar of pickles. King David likes peanut butter. And pickles."

"Is he going to bid on your basket?" Johanna asked.

Susanna nodded. Susanna's would probably be the only lunch container with a crooked letter *S* scrawled backward in inkberry juice. Susanna had marked her basket last summer. The red juice had stained the wicker and no amount of scrubbing could remove her initial.

"What are you going to eat with your peanut butter and pickles?" Rebecca opened the refrigerator door, removed several pieces of fried chicken, wrapped them in foil and tucked them into Susanna's basket. "Do you have napkins and knives and forks?"

Susanna eyed the lunch basket warily. "Don't need them."

"Just in case, Susanna-Banana." Rebecca smiled warmly at her younger sister as she added silverware, napkins and two apples to the container. "David might be hungry."

"Maybe," Susanna said grudgingly. "He likes raisins, too. Raisins are good."

"They are good," Hannah agreed. She reached up into a cabinet and found a box of golden raisins. She held them out, and Susanna's mouth puckered. "You know you like raisins, too," Hannah coaxed.

Susanna opened the basket and pushed the raisins inside. Laboriously, she fastened the lid. "Put it in the buggy," she said. "That's enough food. King David likes peanut butter best."

As she watched her daughter trudge out the door, Hannah wondered if it had been a mistake to allow Susanna to put together a supper basket. But where did she draw the line between protecting her daughter and making Susanna's and her own life even more difficult? Refusing Susanna would have been hurtful. Susanna was a part of the community, and it was natural that she'd want to do what other girls did. The trouble was, no matter what Anna and Jezzy said, she wasn't like other girls. And letting her believe that she was might be the cruelest act of all.

Albert parked his truck behind two others along the road near the Seven Poplars schoolhouse. A horse and buggy was just turning into the driveway, and dozens of black buggies were lined up in the field. A sack race was taking place on the far side of the school, and children, mostly Amish, were playing on the swing set and see-saw, and bouncing on a large, black trampoline. Adults stood talking in small groups while young women carried pies to a long table shaded by a white canvas canopy.

Albert wasn't sure why he was here. Well, he *did* know why. He was here for the good food. And maybe to say hello to Hannah. He just wasn't certain if the decision to come was wise.

Saturday, when they'd gone down to the alpaca farm, it had been Susanna who had invited him to the school picnic. When he'd tried to make an excuse not to come, Hannah had assured him that he'd be welcome and told him that there would be homemade pies for sale as well as jellies, pickles and other home-canned delicacies. She knew his weak spot for home-cooked goodies. He loved pie, and he would walk a mile for real strawberry jam.

It had been a trying day. He'd been called out early that morning to sew up a calf that had been attacked by a stray dog. After that, there had been a young heifer with mastitis and two more urgent cases that had taken up the entire afternoon. Somehow, he'd managed to miss lunch and go all day on three cups of coffee and a stale donut that he'd found in the back of his breadbox.

Seeing the Amish and Mennonite families gathered took Albert back to his own Mennonite childhood. He'd attended a rural schoolhouse only a little larger than this one, and he'd been fortunate enough to grow up in a farming community where most folks didn't count their happiness by how much money they made. He hadn't realized then how fortunate he was or how wealthy he was in the things that mattered. He'd been caught up in dreams of a wider world, and as a teenager, he'd desperately wanted to go to a bigger school, to travel to other parts of the country, to own a television and a truck. Funny, now that he had almost everything he'd ever imagined, those material objects didn't seem as important as he'd expected.

There was something to be said for a slower pace of life, one in which a man or a woman could live closer to the land and nearer to God. He remembered telling his father that if he ever got off the farm, he'd never plow another row again. But, sometimes, on a warm spring day, when the air smelled of growing things and the sun felt warm on his face, his hands itched to wrap around the handles of a horse-drawn cultivator.

*I must be having a midlife crisis,* Albert thought. He considered himself a man of faith. He attended church and Bible study regularly, and he never failed to pitch in to raise money for a good cause or to lend a hand when someone needed it.

He never closed his eyes at night without a period of contemplation and prayer, and he tried to live according to the principles of his faith. Still, he was restless.

As much as he loved his work, and as close as he felt to John and his new family, it wasn't enough. Albert always felt as if there was something he was supposed to do that he'd left undone. He'd never considered himself to be a morose person or a selfish one; he hoped he wasn't being selfish by not being happy with the blessings that God had bestowed on him.

The alpacas, now they were something that got him excited. He'd had such a good time on Saturday when he, 'Kota, Hannah, Irwin and Susanna had gone to make the final arrangements to buy the animals. That night, he'd lain awake for hours thinking about the smell of the alpacas, the soft texture of their fleece and the sounds they made.

A tap on the cab of his truck yanked Albert from his reverie. He looked over to see Hannah's Irwin grinning at him. Irwin was a tall, lanky kid with stiff, corn shock hair, a wide mouth and a plain face. Despite the brief stint that Irwin had worked at the veterinary clinic that hadn't panned out, Albert liked him. Maybe, he saw something of himself in the boy. Sooner or later, Albert was sure, Irwin would find direction, and then Hannah's patient care and affection would prove worthwhile.

Albert opened the truck door. "Hello, Irwin."

"Hurry up, or you'll miss the supper-basket auction." Irwin pointed. "See. People are gathering around the tables."

"I wasn't planning on bidding." Albert got out of the truck and followed the boy across the grass. "Thought maybe I'd buy a rhubarb pie if there are any for sale."

Irwin waited for him to catch up. "Didn't guess you were. But…" He leaned close and whispered, "Lovina packed her supper in Hannah's basket."

Albert raised his eyebrows.

Irwin grinned. "Food will be good because Anna made it, but Lovina…" He grimaced. "I think Jason Peachy is going to try and win the bid, thinking it's Hannah's. He's got his eye on her. Won't he be surprised when Lovina is who he sits down to supper with?"

Albert knew Jason Peachy, a middle-aged widower with three teenage boys. The man owned a hundred-acre farm over near Black Bottom. Albert didn't have much of an opinion of him. But the man didn't have the best setup for the number of hogs he was raising. He'd built his pigpens in a low spot. Not productive cropland, but not a good place for animals, either.

"I didn't know that Hannah was looking to

get married again," Albert commented. As soon as the words were out of his mouth, he wondered why he'd spoken them. It wasn't his concern if Hannah was looking for a husband. Why wouldn't she be? She was still young; she had a lot to offer a man. And it was their way, the Old Order Amish. Frankly, he was surprised she'd stayed single this long.

The teen shrugged. "She'll listen to the bishop sooner or later. He's been telling her she's mourned Jonas too long."

Albert frowned. "The bishop thinks that's *his* business?"

"Everything's his business. He's the bishop. A woman *should* be married."

Something about the careless way the boy was talking about his foster mother rankled Albert, but he held his tongue. He'd known Irwin long enough to realize that he loved Hannah and meant no harm.

"She owns that big farm and she's a good cook," Irwin went on. "Lots of men would want to be her husband, even if she is strong-minded and old."

"Only a fifteen-year-old would call Hannah old," Albert muttered to himself.

Irwin didn't seem to hear or didn't bother to reply. Instead he pointed to a sorry-looking basket at the end of the table. The wicker had seen better days and the catch that held the lid down had broken and was tied with navy blue yarn. *Hannah's,* he mouthed silently and then he motioned toward a knot of young men.

Standing in the center was red-faced, gray-bearded Jason Peachy. He was a short, stocky man wearing a green shirt and black trousers. The man had small, pale blue eyes and his salt-and-pepper brows were thick. The man saw him and turned away.

A group of white *kapps* came into view, chattering women all moving together like a flock of birds. Albert could hear Hannah's distinctive voice in their midst and wondered what she was laughing at. She was a cheerful person, someone whom it was impossible not have a good time with. He just couldn't see her with a man like Jason Peachy. And he couldn't see her happy with all those pigs. That many were bound to cause a stink, no matter how careful a farmer was to keep his pens clean. No, Jason wasn't the husband for her, and if she asked his opinion, he'd be glad to give it.

Hannah's son-in-law Samuel Mast was holding up a basket. When the crowd didn't quiet down, he urged them to in a good-natured way. Albert liked Samuel. He'd been as surprised as everyone else when Samuel had asked Anna to be his wife. He was some years older than she was, and most folks thought to see him courting Hannah. If Hannah had to remarry, Albert hoped it would be someone like Samuel, someone who could truly appreciate her for the fine woman she was.

"What am I bid for this next supper basket?" Samuel called. He lifted the lid and looked inside, making a show of smelling the delicious food. Albert saw that the basket's handle was wrapped with green willow switches.

One of Zack Byler's sons started the bid off at five dollars. Samuel shook his head, saying that he couldn't think of letting the basket go for such a puny amount. He reminded the crowd that this was a school fund-raiser and he was here to accept serious offers. Everyone laughed at the Byler boy as he raised his own bid to ten dollars. Bidding picked up and the basket eventually went to Preacher Caleb for twenty-two dollars.

Albert didn't need Irwin's whisper to tell him that Caleb was Rebecca Yoder's intended. Rebecca would have been heartbroken if anyone else had won her basket. Of course, just the thought that anyone would really challenge Caleb wasn't feasible. The Amish liked a good joke, but they were rarely unkind. The chances were that Samuel had put the Byler boy up to bidding in the first place. But all ended well, and a blushing Rebecca went off happily to share supper with the man who would soon be her husband.

One after another the baskets on the table under the trees were auctioned off. Irwin drifted away with his friends, and Albert's clients, both Amish and English, exchanged greetings with him. Albert was polite, but wasn't feeling as sociable as usual. For some reason his attention remained fixed on the basket Hannah had actually packed.

Samuel kept up a steady patter of auctioneer's jests and taunting, and prices held steady at an average of twenty dollars per supper. Then Samuel produced a basket that appeared as if some child had drawn a snake on it in red poster paint.

"What am I bid for this one?" he asked. Again, he opened the basket, peered inside and pretended to inhale the aromas of wonderful food.

But, to Albert's surprise, no one raised a hand to bid on the sorry little basket. Not a single hand went up. Albert was tempted to offer something, just so that the girl or woman who'd prepared it wouldn't be hurt. Just when he started to move toward the table, the crowd parted and the King boy trudged through to the edge of the table. In one hand, he held a crumpled dollar bill.

"That's mine!" Susanna Yoder cried from the group of women on the far side of the tables. "My basket! Buy that one!"

"Dol-ler," David pronounced. David's father came to stand beside him and the young man smiled. "Susanna's basket," he said waving the dollar again.

"Make that twenty-one." Ebben King handed his son a larger bill.

"Sold to young David King for twenty-one dollars," Samuel declared.

David seemed frozen to the spot. A wide smile spread across his round face and he nodded. "I bought it," he declared loudly. "My Susanna's basket."

Samuel handed over the basket and David proudly carried it away with a giggling Susanna trailing in his wake.

Albert glanced at Hannah, standing among her daughters. His smile faded as he caught the hint of worry in Hannah's expression. Not much she could do about it, he thought. The two youngsters seemed smitten with each other. But he could understand why Hannah had grave reservations about what might come from Susanna's innocent romance.

"What have we here?" Samuel said, drawing the crowd's attention back to the auction. When Albert looked at the basket he was holding, he saw that it was the battered one with the yarn closing. *Hannah's basket.*

"Fifteen dollars," someone offered.

From the back came another bid. "Seventeen!"

"Eighteen," Samuel's boy, Rudy, called.

"No fair," said an onlooker. "He's too young. Admit it, Samuel. He's bidding for you."

Samuel laughed and shrugged. "I've got to eat, too," he admitted. "And I've got a big family to feed."

Jason Peachy threw up his hand. "Twenty-five dollars!"

Albert's stomach clenched. This wasn't the way it was supposed to go. Why were men bidding on a supper everyone was supposed to believe belonged to Lovina Yoder? Had Irwin spilled the secret to the whole crowd?

Samuel laughed. "Twenty-five dollars is the bid. Do I hear twenty-six?"

"It's supper," Rudy said, "Not a whole cow."

Laughter followed.

"Twenty-five once," Samuel called. "Twenty-five twice."

Samuel glanced at Jason Peachy. The pig farmer looked as if his prize sow had just taken first place at the Delaware State Fair. Albert couldn't stand it. "Fifty dollars!" he shouted.

"Sold!" Samuel proclaimed.

# *Chapter Seven*

One minute Hannah was standing with her grandchild on her hip, thoroughly enjoying the supper auction, the next, the eyes of the entire community were on her. Jason Peachy was bidding on her supper basket. And from the sly winks Jason threw her way between bids, he was all too aware that it was her basket and not her mother-in-law's.

Hannah retrieved baby Rose's rag doll, catching it just before it fell from the toddler's hand. In an effort to cover her surprise that she'd been caught in her ruse, Hannah gave all her attention to the child. She adjusted the baby's cap and murmured endearingly to her in *Deitsch*.

Hannah was tempted to chuckle. *Jason Peachy was interested in courting her?* Anna met her gaze and glanced away with a suppressed giggle. Anna knew her too well. One exchanged look was all it took for them to each know what the other was thinking.

*Jason Peachy.* Well, there was a fly in the buttermilk. While she'd been acquainted with Jason for years, Hannah hadn't suspected that he might be sweet on her. He was a widower and near to her age, but the man had only three teenage sons, which was a small family for an Old Order Amish man. She would have thought he'd be interested in a younger woman than her. Someone who could bear him more children and be up to the tasks of working day and night to keep his household running.

He was a somber man, a farmer and a faithful member of another church district in the county. She'd known his wife, Iris, from a shared quilting project. Sadly, Iris had died of cancer the previous fall and Hannah, along with most of the community, attended her funeral. His farm was near Oak Point School, an area known as Black Bottom—low and woody ground. Hannah's sister-in-law Martha, who kept tabs on all eligible bachelors in the county for her daughter, Dorcas, had remarked recently that Jason Peachy hadn't married until he was in his mid-thirties, which was why he didn't have grown children yet.

Hannah's first thought was that Jason hadn't allowed enough time to pass before looking to remarry, but men were helpless creatures without a wife to tend to their needs. She remembered that Iris had been sick for a long time, and mourning periods were often relaxed when needs were to be met. But what was Martha thinking? Jason was too old and set in his way for Dorcas, who was close in age to Johanna.

Still, Hannah thought, her niece wouldn't be the first young woman to take a husband old enough to be her father. For the Old Order Amish, marriage was considered a practical matter of faith and family as much as a romantic attachment. She'd been fortunate enough to have both in Jonas, but not every woman could expect that. And, poor Dorcas had to marry *someone*.

Jason was a perfectly respectable man, even if he did raise pigs for a living. Pigs were never Hannah's favorite animals, but it would be silly to reject a man because of what livestock he raised. Or so she would reason if she had decided she was ready to remarry, which she hadn't. Or, if she favored Jason Peachy, which she didn't, and wanted to cause even more discord between her and Martha. Why in the name of sweet strawberries hadn't the man had the good sense to bid on Dorcas's basket instead of hers? Surely he knew that Martha had her eye on him; everyone else in the county knew it.

All those thoughts tumbled through her mind in the short time it took Samuel to decide that the bid on her basket was as high as it was going to go and call out "Twenty-five once, twenty-five twice…"

*Martha's going to be mad enough bite green grapes and spit out wasps,* Hannah thought as she bounced giggling Rose on her hip and waited to hear Samuel declare, "Sold to Jason Peachy!"

Instead, another voice—Albert Hartman's voice— stunned her by shouting, "Fifty dollars!"

Hannah was so shocked that she nearly dropped Rose. "Here." She pushed the wide-eyed girl into Anna's arms. "Take the baby."

Hannah had never been prone to light-headed nonsense, but suddenly she felt positively giddy. Why had Albert bid on her basket? People would be gossiping about it for months. Then a merry notion came into her head. *Albert's rescued you from Jason Peachy and his pigs.*

Just behind her, Martha remarked sharply in *Deitsch.* "Has Albert Hartman lost his mind? What does he want with Hannah's basket?"

*"Mam?"* Even sensible Anna was shocked. Her eyes were wider than Rose's. "You can't share supper with Albert. He's not one of us. How would it look?"

Hannah's sense of humor surfaced, and she barely stifled a most improper response. Anna was right, of course. She should have been put out with Albert for getting her in this pickle, but all she could think of was how much more enjoyable sharing supper with him would be than eating with Jason Peachy. She wouldn't have to listen to talk of the price of pork or of Jason's plans for a new sty. She and Albert would sit with Anna and her family and he could tell them about the imminent arrival of the alpacas and discuss the details of settling them in on her property.

*"Mam."* Two bright splotches of color tinted Anna's cheeks. "People are whispering." She motioned toward the crowd standing near the auction table.

Hannah rolled her eyes. "Nonsense, daughter. Albert was your father's friend and he knows everyone in the community on a first-name basis. He couldn't have guessed it was my basket."

"And why not?" Anna asked. "Everyone else apparently knows, thanks to Irwin's big mouth."

Hannah waved away Anna's intimation. "I'm sure Albert just wanted to support the school." Or had he bought it knowing it was her basket? Knowing he would be able to share supper with her. The notion was not altogether displeasing. In fact, it was deliciously wicked. And then she had a second notion. Who would have thought that her basket would bring more money than any other for the school?

*Hochmut,* Hannah chided herself. Pride was often the sin of which she'd found herself guilty.

But who was she to complain when the children of Seven Poplars would benefit? Albert's fifty dollars would buy good used math books for her eighth-graders, and they were sorely in need of them. The old ones had been used for so long that they were held together with prayer and duct tape. So what if Albert wasn't Amish? It wasn't as if he was asking her to walk out with him. What was one supper on the ground between old friends?

She felt someone staring at her and raised her gaze to collide with Jason's. He was standing at the edge of the cluster of men, arms folded across his ample belly, his sun-burned features creased in disapproval.

Hannah smiled and fluttered her hand in a gesture that she'd seen Aunt Jezzy use a hundred times. It meant, I'm sorry, it's not my fault. Truthfully, what Hannah really wanted to convey was, *Don't frown at me, you old goat. If you wanted my basket that badly, you should have outbid him.*

*Lord help me,* she thought. *I am truly lacking in charity.*

*"Mam."* Anna's insistent tone broke through Hannah's musing. "What will Caleb think?"

She pursed her lips. Caleb was the new preacher, and her soon-to-be son-in-law. She certainly didn't want to cause a problem for Rebecca or Caleb. More was expected of the families of the church elders. Certain moral standards had to be upheld for the good of the community. "If Albert's planning to stay for the picnic, we'll eat with you and Samuel and the children," Hannah answered.

All this fuss was probably over nothing. Albert might not have realized that he was supposed to share the meal with her. She chuckled. "Be at ease, daughter. Your husband doesn't look put out," she said quietly to Anna. "And he's our deacon."

Samuel was grinning at Albert as he passed the supper basket. "That will be fifty dollars, hard money."

"Will you take a check?" Albert appeared slightly embarrassed.

Samuel laughed. "I suppose we'll have to." He waved toward Hannah. "I hope you've made enough food. Albert has a reputation for having a big appetite."

"So I've heard." Hannah's giddiness made her heart race, but she smiled at Albert as if he were one of her errant pupils. She could feel all her neighbors looking at her, watching to see how she would react. "Well, Samuel," she called back. "You'd better hope that I've packed enough food, because we're eating with you and Anna. If I didn't, you might have to go hungry."

Samuel laughed.

*At least Martha can't say I stole Dorcas's beau,* Hannah thought with satisfaction.

A good-natured Amish mason in a Lincoln green, short-sleeved shirt stepped to the front of the onlookers and clapped his big hands together once. "Get on with the auction, Samuel," he urged. "Albert's not the only one who's hungry."

*"Ya,"* Martha urged, tugging a reluctant Dorcas along with her toward the basket table. "I see at least five more supper baskets still waiting to be sold."

Shyly, carrying Hannah's basket in both hands, Albert walked toward her. The women drew aside to let him pass, all eyes on him. Hannah smiled at him. She would not provide the gossips more to whisper about by acting as if she had something to hide.

"What have you done, Albert?" she teased. He grinned, and she decided that he really did have a very pleasant face.

"I hope I didn't upset anyone's buggy." He glanced over his shoulder and lowered his voice conspiratorially. "And I hope Jason doesn't take it to heart, but I didn't get any lunch today, and… and I thought that a homemade supper made by Hannah Yoder was just what I needed."

She arched one eyebrow. "How did you know I made the food inside? It's my mother-in-law's basket."

He grimaced. "Irwin."

"I was afraid of that. Shall we join the family?"

She motioned toward Anna. "She and Samuel have laid their picnic supper out in the shade on the far side of the schoolhouse."

"I'd like that," Albert agreed. "I thought we could share with Grace and 'Kota, too. They're here somewhere, and I imagine that they're hungry, too."

"Of course. I think they were already planning to join us." Hannah's smile was genuine. She felt relieved. Albert had known which basket was hers, but he'd only bid on it because he liked her cooking and he wanted to provide for Grace and 'Kota. Not even Bishop Atlee could find fault with an outsider sharing a meal with so many of the family included.

"It was kind of you to contribute so much to our school fund," she said, as she fell into step with him. "And I'll be glad to see my daughter and grandson."

'Kota was her daughter Grace's son by her first marriage, not her grandson by blood, but certainly by heart. Since Grace and Albert's nephew, John, were Mennonite and not Amish, 'Kota didn't attend the Seven Poplars School. Public school wouldn't let out until June, but after that, he'd be spending much of the summer on the farm with Hannah and Susanna while Grace studied for her degree as a veterinary technician at the local college.

"John couldn't make it?" Hannah asked as they rounded the corner of the schoolhouse. She could feel heat in her cheeks, but had no idea why she was blushing.

Albert shook his head. "No. We have a couple of post-op patients at the clinic and he volunteered to stay and watch over them. You know how seriously John takes his work."

"I do," Hannah assured him. She surveyed the three quilts that Anna had spread on the ground earlier. Samuel and Anna's children were there as were Miriam and Charley, sitting among dishes and bowls and plates of food. She'd expected to find Susanna and David, but they were nowhere in sight. "I wonder where Susanna got to?" she murmured. With the auction almost over, other families were gathering to eat on the softball field, under the trees and on the schoolhouse porch.

"I could go and look for them if you like," Albert offered.

*"Ne."* Hannah shrugged. "I'm sure they're with David's parents. Susanna knows better than to wander off."

Ruth came toward them carrying one of her twin boys. Hannah saw her son-in-law Eli with the other boy coming behind her. "Are you eating with us, too?" Hannah asked.

*"Ya.* And Johanna and Roland and the children," Ruth said. She nodded a greeting to Albert

before glancing from the supper basket he was carrying to Hannah. "Eli wants to talk to you about Irwin."

Hannah grimaced. "What's he done now?"

Ruth laughed and held up her son for Hannah to nuzzle. "Not a thing. Eli has a new contract and needs help at the shop. He was hoping you could spare Irwin to give him a hand."

"Of course," Hannah answered. "If he can use him. Irwin needs direction." Neither of them was unkind enough to say that the boy wasn't much help on the farm. "I think these two have grown since I've seen them."

"In two days?" Ruth laughed and handed the baby over.

Hannah squeezed him and inhaled the sweet baby scent of her youngest grandson. Ruth had just sewn the twins new baby caps and gowns. They were beautiful babies, but had yet to grow much hair. Hannah thought Luke's might grow in dark like their father's, but Adam was definitely a redhead.

"I heard all about the alpacas," Ruth said to Albert. "It's all my nieces and nephews have been talking about. When are they coming?"

"This weekend, I hope." He placed Hannah's basket on the nearest blanket. "There's Grace." He waved. "Over here, Grace."

She waved back. "Uncle Albert. *Mam.* Hi,

everyone!" Grace called as she crossed the school-yard to join them. 'Kota trailed behind her, but perked up when he saw his cousins. Soon, they were all gathered for a moment of silent thanks before the meal.

Johanna and her husband joined them and their little ones, laughing and talking excitedly, scattered among their cousins. Food was passed around between Hannah's daughters, their husbands and children without regard to whose box, bag or basket it came from. Within minutes, everyone was eating and sharing the week's news, Albert included. Roland was eager to hear about the alpacas and the children kept chiming in, all excited about the arrival at their grandmother's farm of the exotic animals.

Charley brought a folding chair and a desk out of the schoolhouse for Lovina, who appeared with the young man who'd successfully bid on her basket. It was Lydia's eighteen-year-old son, Elmer, much to everyone's delight. Elmer was one of Irwin's cousins, and Irwin took great pleasure in teasing him over his supper partner. No doubt, he'd bid on the basket at Samuel's request. Samuel held Elmer to the bargain until the food was parceled out, then said that he and Irwin were free to go and eat with their friends. The teenagers didn't need to be told twice.

"Don't forget," Eli called after Irwin. "Be at the shop at eight sharp tomorrow morning."

Irwin turned and waved. "*Ya,* I'll be there."

"I'm thinking this might be good for Irwin," Eli said to Hannah. "He seemed interested in assembling the kitchen cabinets when he came by last week."

"It will be a blessing if you can teach him a trade." Hannah munched on a carrot stick that was sweet and crispy. "Maybe woodwork is something he has a feel for."

"He'll find his way," *Grossmama* Lovina injected. "He's young and foolish, but they all are at that age. You should have seen what a woodenhead my Jonas was. And look at him now." Surrounded by family, *Grossmama* Lovina was content, even jovial. She smiled and patted Samuel's arm. "A *gut* boy, my Jonas."

Albert glanced questioningly at Hannah.

She leaned close and whispered. "Sometimes Lovina's mind wanders. She thinks Samuel is Jonas. He was her only son, and she has never gotten over his passing."

Albert nodded. "She's right," he agreed. "Jonas was a good man, one of the finest I've ever known."

"He was a good husband and a good father. He would have enjoyed the picnic today." Hannah smiled, feeling nostalgic, but not sad. She really didn't feel so sad anymore. It was true that time healed sorrow. "Jonas never missed a school frolic."

Johanna's Katy sat down beside Hannah. "*Mam* says I can go to school next fall," she announced. "I want to go to school. I want a pink lunchbox."

Hannah smiled at her granddaughter and wiped a smear of baked beans off the child's chin. "Black it will have to be, my sweet, but maybe your mama will find you a pink thermos to go inside."

Katy grinned, then her eyes widened as she caught sight of a pile of treats. "Can I have a popcorn ball?"

"You may." Hannah dug in her basket and came up with six. "Pass them out to the other children," she said. "And if there aren't enough to go around, Aunt Ruth made more. Hers are rainbow-colored."

"Sixteen dollars," *Grossmama* Lovina repeated loudly for the third time. "That Beachy boy paid sixteen dollars for my basket. He didn't know it was mine. Thought he was getting some young gal's." She laughed so hard that she nearly choked on her fried chicken.

Hannah paused, fork in hand, and looked around at her family. She had been truly blessed in her children and their husbands, her grandchildren and her friends. *Thank You, God,* she offered silently. What more could she ask for? Then her gaze drifted to Miriam, who was watching her. There was something in her daughter's eyes that concerned Hannah. Was it worry? Worry for her? Lately, she'd noticed this look on her daughters' faces more often than she cared to admit.

Maybe the bishop and her friends were right. Maybe, so long as she remained single, her daughters felt responsible for her. She didn't want that. It would be natural when and if she reached Lovina's age, but for now, while she was strong, healthy and active, they didn't need to worry about her needs. After Rebecca's wedding, she would stop her dithering and think seriously about remarrying. It was expected of an Amish woman in her position. It was the right thing to do. Surely, there was someone in this community or another with whom she would be content to share the rest of her life. But, she decided finally, she would not leave. Her roots were sunk too deep. She would take a new husband and she would give him the respect and affection he needed, but she would not move away from her children.

She would not.

"Do you think you could?" Albert asked. "Would it be permitted?"

Hannah blinked. Had she been wool-gathering again? "I'm sorry. What did you ask me?"

Albert used a cloth napkin to wipe his mouth.

He had such a sincere, kind face. "I was wondering if you would like to come with me to bring the alpacas home."

Hannah didn't have to think before she responded. "I'd like that. You think it will be Saturday?" There were questions she wanted to ask the man who'd raised them, habits and likes and dislikes of individual animals that Albert might not think important. In her experience, each animal was different, and it was most important that the herd leader, the female that Albert had mentioned, be happy in her new home.

"I'm hoping for Saturday, but I'll let you know as soon as I confirm."

"*Ya,* I will come," she said. "I'll bring Susanna, too, if that's all right."

"Of course," Albert said. "I think she had a good time before."

"She did. She had a wonderful time, and so did I," Hannah confessed cheerfully. "She'll be so excited to know we're going with you to pick up the animals." *Me, too,* Hannah thought. Now that the school frolic was almost over, she would have that to look forward to.

Of course, Rebecca's wedding would be a happy day for them all. But the wedding meant a lot to do and many things to plan for. Guests would be coming from out of state to stay with her, and she and the girls would have tons of food to make. Going with Albert to bring home the alpacas, that would be a day of fun with nothing to do but enjoy herself. She couldn't wait.

## Chapter Eight

Hannah tied her *kapp* strings and picked up her purse. She was so annoyed with Susanna that she had to keep her lips pressed tightly together to keep from saying something that she'd regret. This was the morning that she and Susanna were supposed to ride to Maryland with Albert to pick up the alpacas. Yesterday, Susanna had been so excited about going, but this morning was a different story.

"Susanna," she muttered under her breath. "What am I going to do with you?"

Rebecca was at Anna's making wedding plans. Susanna had gone next door to Ruth's to return a bag of sugar that they'd borrowed earlier in the week. She was supposed to come right back, but instead, she'd apparently met David at the end of the lane. The two of them had gone to Milford in a van with David's mother and older sister.

Hannah wouldn't even have known it if Charley hadn't stopped by to tell her.

"Susanna said it would be all right with you," Charley had said. "David said they were going to have pizza."

So much for keeping a tighter rein on her, Hannah thought wryly.

What had Susanna been thinking? If she'd decided that she would rather go and have pizza with David than go to get the alpacas, the right thing would have been to come home and ask permission.

Once again, Hannah felt the weight of being a single parent. "If Jonas were here," she murmured. But that was self-pity. Jonas wasn't here. Her beloved husband had been called home to the Lord, and she'd been left behind. It was her job to make the best of her life and to care for her children, as Jonas would have expected her to. Usually, she did, but she'd hit an unexpected obstacle. What was she going to do with Susanna?

Albert was going to be here any moment. Strictly speaking, it wouldn't be proper for her to go off for the day with Albert without a chaperone. But she'd been looking forward it, and she wanted to help fetch the animals. Between teaching school and her housework, she rarely got a day off to do something fun like this. It wasn't fair that Susanna could spoil her outing.

In the end, she decided to go anyway. Being in a truck with Albert wasn't the same as entertaining him in her home. As long as they were in public, where anyone could see that they weren't misbehaving, she didn't see how it could raise any eyebrows. Jonah had always said, "Misdeeds start in the heart." She was going with a trusted friend to help bring home animals to the farm. If anyone else wanted to think the less of her for it, then that was their affair.

"Where's Susanna?" Albert asked as he opened the truck door for Hannah. "I thought she was coming with us."

Hannah shrugged and gave him a wry look. "So did I, but she's given me the slip again. She went off for the day with David and his parents, something about pizza." She climbed up into the vehicle, and he closed the door behind her.

As he walked back to the driver's side, Albert glanced at the horse trailer he'd borrowed from a client to bring the alpacas home. He had experience in pulling trailers, but not one as large or new as this. He could only imagine what it cost, and it made him a little nervous to be responsible for it. But, he'd been stuck. There was nothing comparable to rent in the area, and his only other solution would have been to pay to have the animals hauled. He'd rather not do that. He didn't want to take any chances with the alpacas' safety, and he knew that he'd be more careful of their well-being than someone being paid to deliver them.

As he got back into the cab, he smiled at Hannah. He was so glad that she was coming, despite her daughter abandoning them. He'd been looking forward to talking with Hannah on the drive, and he was eager to have her participate in the alpaca project at every step. "I had a really good time at the school picnic," he said to her.

She smiled back at him, and he was struck again by what an attractive woman Hannah Yoder was. Her modest green dress, black apron and white *kapp* all appeared freshly washed and ironed. She looked so wholesome. Her hair was rolled into a kind of a bun and tucked up under her *kapp,* but what he could see was a soft, reddish-brown that matched her large, brown, intelligent eyes. Hannah really didn't look a day over thirty-five, although he supposed she had to be closer to his age.

Albert started the truck and carefully pulled the vehicle in a wide circle before exiting the long drive. He didn't say anything until after he pulled out onto the blacktop and drove past the chair shop. "I have to confess, I didn't come to the fund-raiser intending to bid on your basket," he explained. "I was just hoping to get some chicken salad and a sweet to take home."

"A pretty expensive supper it turned out to be." She chuckled. "I'll admit that I was surprised." She glanced at him from under long, thick lashes and he saw the mischief sparkling there. "You surprised a lot of people, Albert. We were the talk of the picnic." She uttered a small sound of amusement. "For about five minutes, until the Beachy boy won my mother-in-law's supper basket. And then the joke was on poor Elmer."

"He was a good sport to bid on her basket. I'm sure someone put him up to it. I hope Lovina wasn't upset that he didn't stay with her for the picnic."

"*Ne,* she wasn't. So long as she has Anna and the children nearby, she's happy."

"She seems content in Anna's household," Albert observed.

One thing that the Amish had in common with his own faith was a strong belief in caring for their own. Among the Mennonites, the elderly— no matter how ill their health—rarely went into nursing care. The Old Order Amish observed the same tradition. He'd never heard of an Amish man or woman being a resident of a nursing home. It made him think of Susanna and others with special needs, and what a good job Hannah had done of making her an integral part of the family.

*"Ya,"* Hannah agreed. "She is. Far happier than she was when she stayed with me. I don't know why, but the two of us always rubbed each other the wrong way. I tried to respect her and to make allowances for her age and the mental losses she's suffered, and I prayed for God to give me patience—something I've always had in short supply. But I wasn't the girl that Lovina wanted for her son, and she never let me forget it."

"Because you were a convert to the Amish church?"

Hannah glanced at him, then away.

He concentrated on the road. "I'm sorry. I didn't mean to pry."

*"Ne."* She shook her head. "It's no secret in the family, that I was once Mennonite or that Lovina never approved of me. My conversion was so long ago that I sometimes forget myself." She smiled, seeming to have drifted off to a time and place far in the past. "Jonas was strong in his faith. We were very much in love, but there was never a question of his leaving. It would have broken his mother's heart, and his sisters'."

"And you? Was it hard for you to leave your own faith?"

She took a moment to answer, as if she were choosing her words carefully. "It was difficult because my family and his both opposed the match so strongly. But becoming Amish and stepping apart from the English world wasn't as bad as you'd think. Jonas and I were meant to be together, and it was the only way."

"And you've been happy in his church?"

She nodded. "I found a peace here that I never knew before. For me, it was the right choice."

"Did your parents learn to accept your decision?"

She sighed. "*Ne,* they didn't. My father was a leader in our church, very strict, very much the head of our household. My mother didn't oppose his wishes. He said that if I became Amish, I was dead to them, and I wasn't welcome in their home." Hannah wiped at the corner of her eye, as if she had something in it, but her voice remained soft and clear. "I tried to see my mother when Ruth was a baby and again before she passed away. Both times, someone alerted my father, and he locked the door. I went to the graveyard. He couldn't prevent that, but it was hurtful, not being able to say goodbye."

"And your father? You never made your peace with him?"

She shook her head. "He went on a mission to Northern Canada several years later, and he died of a heart attack." She sighed again. "I pray for them both every night, and I am certain we'll be reunited in heaven."

"Brothers? Sisters?"

"One sister, much older. She's dead, too. My mother was forty-four when I was born. But I can't complain. I was blessed with seven loving daughters, eight including Grace, and they have added to my joy with husbands and children. And I have the whole Seven Poplars Community. Sometimes we rub and pinch each other like a new leather shoe, but they are all family."

"You make me envious when you put it that way." Albert gripped the steering wheel a little tighter as he approached a four-way stop. "I was foolish not to have married when I was a young man. I could have had children of my own."

She chuckled. "When you were a *young* man? You're hardly a graybeard, Albert."

"Fifty-three my last birthday."

She spread her hands. "As I said, no graybeard. And you're right. You should have married. God never intended for men to live alone."

"Or women?"

She laughed. "You have me there. Caught in my own tangle of yarn. But, seriously, Albert, many women would find you attractive. You have a good character. You are respected, and you could provide for a wife and family. You could marry. You could marry a woman who could give you children."

Albert felt the back of his neck growing warm. Why was he talking to Hannah about such personal subjects, and how had they gotten from her conversion to the Amish to his regrets about not having children? He wasn't a man who discussed his personal life. He exhaled slowly. But Hannah was so easy to be with, so easy to talk to, that he'd let down his guard.

"Something I wanted to ask you," he said, abruptly changing the subject as he made a left turn onto a larger road. "At the school picnic, when your little granddaughter said that she wanted a pink lunchbox, you told her that it would have to be black. Do you mind if I ask why? If pink makes a child happy, why shouldn't she be allowed to have it?"

"Maybe that's a question you should be asking Bishop Atlee or my new, soon-to-be son-in-law."

By the animated tone of her voice, Albert knew Hannah wasn't offended. He pressed her. "I'm asking you. Why do you think it would be wrong?"

"It isn't a question of pink or black or of Katy's happiness. Believe me, if Katy gets a new lunchbox for school, she'll be happy. There's nothing wrong with black and it will look just like everyone else's lunchbox at school. Black is Plain. We're plain. If Johanna bought Katy a pink lunchbox, other little girls who didn't have one might feel hurt. The pink lunchbox would make Katy different."

"Better than the other girls?"

"*Ne,* Albert, not better. Just different. Our faith teaches us that what is important is family, community. Like a bee amid thousands in a beehive, we each have a place. We don't need to stand out as individuals. God sees each of us as we truly are, for what we are inside, in our hearts. Katy is a beautiful soul. She doesn't need a pink lunchbox. She is special in His eyes just as she is." Hannah nodded in conviction. "And the pink wouldn't make her happy if it was different. Little girls want to be exactly like their friends and the bigger girls who are there to guide them. It would be no favor to her if we let her think that we would indulge every whim that pops into her head."

Albert mulled over what Hannah had said before speaking. "I see what you're saying, but 'Kota has a superhero on his lunchbox, and I don't see that it has hurt him any."

"That's fine for 'Kota. He goes to school with children who carry all kinds of lunch containers. No one will point him out as different." She smiled. "More than they already do because he is such a kind boy."

"And smart," Albert added. "Top of his class. I wouldn't be surprised to see him in vet school someday."

"If it's what he wants, it would be a good thing," Hannah agreed. "I know John would be pleased."

They drove for several miles in comfortable silence. After a few minutes, Albert said, "There's this place not far ahead. They have make really good sausage sandwiches. Would you mind if we stopped there?"

"Don't tell me you missed breakfast again." She chuckled at him.

"I won't." He grinned. "But I will admit to being hungry."

"You're always hungry," she teased. "Of course, we can stop for you to have something."

"They have other stuff," he suggested. "Good coffee and delicious pie."

"Pie and coffee? I think I'd like that."

Albert's grin grew wider.

As they sat in the comfortable booths in the modest restaurant, Hannah found herself chatting away as easily with Albert as she might one of her daughters. Albert was clearly a smart man; he was an animal doctor, after all. But he had common sense and a genuine concern for other people. She hadn't felt this much at ease with a man since Jonas had passed away. Not that a beloved husband and a simple friend of the family could be considered in the same way, but as much as she valued her sons-in-law and other men in the community, Albert was special. He made her laugh, and allowed for her beliefs.

When she accepted his offer to have something to eat at Annie's Sausage Corner, she'd agreed on the condition that she pay for her own food. She didn't have to explain that letting him treat her would be stepping over the line, a line she'd already smudged by coming with him today without a chaperone.

It was cool inside the restaurant. There were few patrons. Hannah thought it must be late for the breakfast crowd and too early for lunch. She ordered iced tea and a slice of blueberry pie with whipped cream. "What time is the farmer expecting us?" she asked after they'd given the waitress their orders.

"He said he would be there all day. I'm supposed to call him fifteen minutes out."

They discussed the feeding schedule for the alpacas, and Albert began to tell her about some of his more interesting animal patients. He'd cared for an armadillo, a deodorized skunk, a mountain lion and a condor with an injured wing. Only the skunk had been his patient here in Delaware. He'd seen the exotic animals when he'd attended veterinary school out west.

"The skunk bit me," he told her. "I find I don't have much sympathy for skunks."

Hannah laughed. "I don't, either. We had one in our henhouse once, and it killed a chicken. Not only that, but we couldn't get the smell out and we had to build a new chicken coop."

The waitress, a middle-aged woman with bright orange lipstick, was pleasant and efficient. She didn't stare or question Hannah about her Amish clothing, and she seemed in no hurry to have them eat, pay the bill and leave the booth for the next customers. Hannah's iced tea was very good, and although she secretly thought her own crust was flakier, she found the pie delicious, too.

"How is Leah?" Albert asked between bites. Despite having already eaten something that morning, he'd ordered a full breakfast, complete with eggs, pancakes, sausage and a white, mealy looking mound of grits that Hannah didn't think looked particularly appetizing. "Have you had a letter recently?"

Hannah nodded. "Just last week, I got two." She explained to Albert that mail delivery was erratic in and out of Leah and Daniel's mission. Daniel was a Mennonite missionary, and he, her daughter and baby grandchild made their home on the edge of the Brazilian rainforest. Albert's church, the same one that Daniel's aunt and uncle belonged to, were strong supporters of Daniel's work. Every year they held a fund-raiser to provide educational and medical supplies for the clinic and school.

"Daniel's been sick with fever again," Hannah said. "It's troublesome. His aunt was hoping he'd come home to be treated, but Leah says the need there is great. Their presence keeps the area from being overrun by farmers wanting free land and cutting down the jungle for pasture for beef cattle." Many of the people that her daughter and son-in-law served were only a generation away from a tribal existence. They were new Christians, and Daniel was afraid if he came back to the States, his congregation would slip away.

"It's selfless work they do, both of them," Albert said. "It can't be an easy life. And I know you miss Leah terribly."

"I do," Hannah admitted. "And I know she misses her home and family, but she feels strongly that God wants her to be there."

"How is Leah's health? And the baby?"

"Both well, thank the Lord. She remains healthy. But they are anxious to have another child." Hannah averted her eyes. How could she have admitted such a private thing to Albert? She, who was usually reserved about sharing family matters? But, if the remark made him uncomfortable, he didn't show it.

"You must be very proud of her," he said. "Of all your daughters."

She sighed. "I am, a fault I can't seem to shake." Their gazes met, and she could see instant understanding in his expression. Hannah rolled her eyes. "Pride is a sin I've prayed to overcome. It's not something a Plain woman should feel."

"But human." Albert reached across the table and covered her hand with his. "Very—"

A warm tingling shot up Hannah's wrist and forearm. She gasped and felt herself blush as she withdrew her hand with as much dignity as she possessed.

"I'm sorry," Albert said quickly. "I didn't mean…" He was turning red, as well.

*"Ne,"* Hannah said. "It's nothing. You were just…" Just what? Like a guilty teenager, she tucked the offending hand under the table and concentrated on the remaining bites of pie.

Albert began to talk very fast about John's search for a pony for 'Kota, and gradually the tension in the air began to dissolve.

*It was just a friendly touch,* Hannah told herself. *It didn't mean anything. Albert didn't do anything wrong.* Stealthily, she glanced around the restaurant at the other customers to see if anyone had noticed. But everyone seemed to be concentrating on their own meals, eating, laughing and chatting. No one had seen the brief touch. There was no need for her or Albert to feel guilty.

But Hannah had never been good at deceiving herself. If Albert reaching for her hand had meant nothing, then why was her heart racing, and why were butterflies fluttering in her stomach? Had she mistakenly given Albert the idea that their friendship was something more?

And more importantly, was it?

# Chapter Nine

Rebecca's wedding day was as beautiful a day as any bride could ask for. It was warm and sunny with clear blue skies and a slight breeze that ruffled the maple leaves over Albert's head. He was seated on the ground in the alpaca pasture with his legs stretched out in front of him and his back against a tree trunk. Although Rebecca and Caleb's ceremony and worship service were being held at Samuel and Anna's house, they'd be joining immediate family and close friends at Hannah's for the midday meal. The dinner would be one long celebration that would stretch into the evening supper when even more family and friends, including non-Amish like Albert, were invited to join them.

Albert had intended to come by early that morning, tend to the alpacas and be well away before the wedding party arrived, but it hadn't turned out that way. He was called out early on an emergency and spent most of the morning in a barn with a client's valuable milk cow. He'd been able to help the animal and the farmer, but he'd been late arriving to feed the alpacas. Normally, Hannah or Irwin could have fed them, but with Rebecca and Caleb's wedding, they had more than enough to do without worrying about his livestock.

It had been two weeks since he'd brought the alpacas to Hannah and they seemed to be slowly settling in. One of the young females was friendly enough to allow him to pet her, but the rest—especially Estrella, the herd leader—still kept a wary distance. He'd thought that if he just sat still and gave her the chance to satisfy her curiosity about him, he might win her confidence. The previous owner had warned him that gaining Estrella's trust wouldn't be easy, because she was protective of her offspring, but once he did, the others would follow her example.

Since getting the animals home to Hannah's, his admiration for them had only grown. He loved watching them, as the llamalike animals interacted with one another. He liked the way their ears went up when something caught their attention, and the way that—if something displeased them, they clustered together amid a chorus of clicks and squeaks and swept away with all the grace of a flock of birds. The alpacas were intelligent. He could see that in their large, expressive eyes and the way they communicated with each other. He was particularly touched by the loving way that Estrella and the others behaved toward the little black cria. Wherever the baby alpaca wandered in the pasture, adults remained nearby, keeping an eye on him and answering his every cry with reassuring clicks.

"I'm not going to hurt your baby," he crooned to Estrella. He'd just sat down for a minute to see if he could coax the cria closer to him. "I wouldn't hurt any of you for all the world." Twice the adventurous little male had ventured almost within arm's reach, and both times, his mother had called him away with a sharp little snort of disapproval. Albert thought that if he could be patient and sit still just a little longer, he'd have the opportunity to stroke the soft fleece and scratch behind the baby alpaca's ears.

The little male thrust out his head and wrinkled his nose, moving closer to Albert, step by step. "That's it," Albert whispered. "Come on, just a little—"

The rattle of buggy wheels in the yard sent the cria racing back to the safety of his mother. Albert looked up in surprise as the whole herd of alpacas trotted to the far end of the pasture and formed a cluster around the baby.

Could it be that late? Hannah had assured him that the service would last until after one, and it was only…Albert checked his watch and grimaced. *No. It couldn't be.* He'd sat here in the pasture that long?

Feeling foolish, he got to his feet and brushed the grass off the back of his pants. He'd make his departure quickly and hope that Hannah wouldn't be put out with him. Things were already awkward enough between them. He didn't want to make matters worse. The Saturday that they'd retrieved the alpacas, they'd pretended that nothing had happened between them when he'd laid his hand on hers at the diner. But they had both been all too aware that it had, and the easy companionship between them had vanished, replaced with a polite tension and uncertainty. The friendship wasn't gone, but it had subtly changed, and he had no idea how to make things right again. He'd barely seen Hannah in the past two weeks. He told himself it was because he was busy with work and she with wedding plans, but he wasn't entirely sure that was true. Was she avoiding him?

He groaned. Would his intrusion on the wedding dinner add to the discomfort between him and Hannah? Why hadn't he paid closer attention to the time?

He hurried across the pasture and let himself

out of the gate beside the stable, taking care to make certain the latch was closed behind him.

Several more buggies were coming up the lane behind the first one. There was no way that he could get out of the yard without being noticed.

He'd been such an idiot when he'd reached out and touched Hannah's hand in the restaurant. They'd been having such a good time. He couldn't remember a day when he'd enjoyed himself more. Taking her hand had felt so right, so natural, but it was *so* wrong. He could see that, looking back. A man didn't touch an Amish woman he wasn't closely related to. What must she have thought of him? He hadn't intended any disrespect. It had been a brief touch, but he couldn't get it out of his head and he couldn't stop remembering how warm and vibrant her hand had felt.

Albert didn't have all that much experience with the opposite sex, not as a young man, and certainly not in recent years, but he knew his own mind. He'd developed an affection for Hannah Yoder, a tender feeling that he'd never felt for another human being. He was afraid now that it was more than friendship, more than respect. After waiting his whole life for God to send him the right match—why had he opened his heart to a woman he couldn't have?

He strode purposefully across the yard toward

his truck and reached it with a sigh of relief, and put his hand on the door handle.

"Albert!"

He turned and forced a smile. "Hannah. How was the wedding?"

Her returning smile answered his question. "Good." She nodded. "Of all the men I could have chosen for my Rebecca, I believe Caleb will make her the happiest."

Hannah's gaze met his, and his heart leaped in his chest. He swallowed, wanting to congratulate her, afraid to break the first warm exchange they'd shared since he'd overstepped his bounds. "I...I'm glad," he mumbled. "I'm sorry. I was just leaving. I didn't expect to be here when..."

Hannah cut off his explanation with a gesture. "I'm so glad you are. I didn't want to bother you, but my friend Sara Yoder needs a vet." She motioned to a plump little woman in a lavender dress and black bonnet getting out of Charley's buggy. "Sara! Over here! This is Albert!"

As the woman walked toward them, Hannah went on to explain the problem. "Sara came for the wedding. Her van driver accidently stepped on her dog's foot. Molly won't put any weight on it, and Sara's afraid it might be broken."

"I'd be glad to take a look," Albert said.

"*Ya*. If you would."

Sara joined them, and Hannah quickly made the introductions.

Sara seemed a pleasant woman in a take-charge way, but Albert could barely take his eyes off Hannah. Maybe things would be all right between them, he thought hopefully. Maybe they could put that awkward moment behind them and go back to being friends. He didn't want to think about losing her.

"If you'd like to bring your pup out to the barn, I can have a look," Albert told Sara, glancing up as more buggies rolled into the barnyard.

"You'll have to excuse me, but I have to run," Hannah told Albert. "We have to have the food out before Rebecca and Caleb get here. "Don't worry, Sara," she reassured her friend. "Albert will take good care of Molly. He's the best."

"I'll see what I can do," he promised. "But if I suspect broken bones, I may have to take her to the clinic for an X-ray."

"Whatever it takes, Albert," Sara said. "I can pay. Molly is dear to me, even if she is just an animal."

"No need to talk about payment." Albert looked at the ground, knowing very well he couldn't just stand here and stare at Hannah. "You're Hannah's guest, and this is a special day for the family."

"Thank you, Albert," Hannah said with another smile. "I knew I could count on you." She started to walk away, then stopped and glanced back over her shoulder. "You are coming for supper with John and Grace and 'Kota tonight, aren't you?"

"I'm not sure if—"

"I won't take no for an answer," Hannah interrupted. "Spare ribs, beef brisket with sauerkraut and dumplings, leg of lamb, *hasenpfeffer,* and more shoofly pie than even you can eat."

Albert didn't know what to say. He'd been thinking of excuses, hadn't been certain that he would come with the family this evening. He didn't want to hurt Rebecca or Caleb's feelings, but he hadn't wanted to make Hannah uncomfortable by his presence.

A smile tilted the corner of Hannah's mouth. "Albert?"

"All right," he answered, knowing when he was beaten. How could anyone refuse Hannah when she was looking at him with those big, beautiful brown eyes? "I'll be here," he said. "Wouldn't miss it."

Twenty minutes later, Albert patted Molly's shaggy head and turned to Sara with a reassuring smile. "No serious damage done," he pronounced. Molly was a tricolored mixed breed, weighing about fifteen pounds, with a sweet nature. "She's more bruised than anything. She should be back to normal in a few days." He picked up the animal and handed her back to her owner.

Molly gave a small sound of pleasure, snuggled down in Sara's arms, and closed her eyes as Sara cradled the dog against her. "Thank you, Albert," she said. "It was kind of you to take the time to see her."

"You obviously take good care of her." The dog's muscle tone and weight were excellent, and he'd observed the thin scar that indicated that she'd been spayed. "Is she up to date on all her shots?"

*"Ya,"* Sara replied. "She is."

"I wish all my clients showed as much care for their animals as you do," he said as they made their way out of the barn. "Well, I hope you enjoy your stay here in Delaware, and have a safe trip back to Wisconsin."

"Albert!" Charley called to him from the driveway. He was unloading two chairs from a wagon. "I've got to go back to Samuel's to pick up Miriam's *grossmama* and the twins. Would you mind carrying these around the house for me? Put them at the bridal table. They're gifts for Rebecca and Caleb."

"No problem," Albert said. The chairs were high-backed Windsors, fashioned of cherry. Ruth's husband, Eli Lapp, was a fine craftsman, so skilled that some of his furniture was sold in shops in Colonial Williamsburg. Albert had never thought much about buying good furniture, but these pieces, with care, would become heirlooms.

He carried the chairs, one in each arm carefully across the lawn to the shaded reception area. He'd never been invited to an Old Order Amish wedding celebration before, but Grace had explained the wedding dinner arrangements to him the previous night.

Just after dawn, volunteers had come to Hannah's to erect seven long tables under the trees on the lawn. If the weather hadn't cooperated, dinner would have had to be held inside, and the guests would have had to eat in shifts, but outside there was room for everyone to sit down at one time. One table, called the *eck,* was set at an angle under a spreading oak and decorated with an antique white-on-white hand-embroidered tablecloth, handmade candies and two fancy cakes. The bridal party, consisting of Rebecca, Caleb and two couples who served as their attendants would be seated there.

Teams of helpers had already set the tables with dishes, glassware and silverware. Now, those same helpers were busy carrying roasted chicken, duck and goose to the tables, along with bowls of mashed potatoes, turnips, green beans, peas and an assortment of yeast rolls and breads. Albert dodged one of the Beachy girls bearing a covered tureen of something that smelled delicious. He placed the two chairs next to four identical ones and looked around for Hannah. Then he wove past a bevy of young mothers with babies and started around the house to where he'd parked his truck.

As he came around the corner, Albert saw another table set with giant containers of lemonade, iced tea and sweet cider, and standing beside it was a smaller one holding empty pitchers. He stopped short, and his mouth gaped in surprise. It wasn't the liquid refreshments that caught his attention, but the young couple standing in front of it, lips locked together.

David King spotted Albert over Susanna's shoulder, gasped and stumbled backward, pulling her with him. The two of them fell against the drinks table, and as Albert darted toward them, one table leg collapsed and table, glass containers, tea, lemonade and cider all came crashing down. Susanna began to wail. David jumped up, looked frantically around and pulled her to her feet.

"Are you hurt?" Albert called, rushing to their sides.

Neither of them answered. Instead, David turned and fled, dragging a sobbing Susanna after him.

"Wait!" Albert looked from the fleeing pair to the wreckage in front of him. A gallon jug of iced tea had rolled, unbroken, across the grass to lodge against a maple tree trunk. An insulated drink cooler had fallen to the ground and was leaking what looked to be lemonade, but the rest of the drinks containers were a total loss.

*"Was is do uff?"* Hannah appeared at Albert's side. "What happened?" she cried, bringing her hands to her head. "Achh. What are we going to do? Rebecca and Caleb are about to be seated at the *eck*. I'll have nothing but water to offer our guests."

"It looks like a table leg gave way." Neither Susanna nor David had appeared to have been hurt in the accident so he didn't think it necessary to tattle on them, at least not just yet. Not now in the midst of the celebration; it would ruin Hannah's day. "Let me handle this," he offered. "Go back to your guests. I'll find you more drinks."

"But how? We used all the tea and lemons in the house."

Albert was afraid Hannah was going to burst into tears. "It's not such a big thing," he soothed, resisting the urge to pat her arm. He'd made that kind of mistake once; he wouldn't do it again. "Go, and don't worry. I'll take care of it."

Hannah clasped her hands together. A wisp of reddish-brown hair had escaped from her *kapp* to fall across her forehead and he found himself wanting to touch it.

"Are you sure?" Despite her obvious capabilities and sensibility, she looked a little lost.

"I've got it under control," he assured her, thinking he would have done anything for her at this moment: fought a bull in a bullfighting ring, wrangled a herd of stampeding horses or walked to California to get more lemons for her lemonade.

She was still holding his gaze with hers.

He smiled and she smiled back and off she hurried.

Albert slipped his cell phone from his pocket. He punched in John's number and explained the emergency. "Ask one of the girls at the office to go for ice, juice, soda—root beer and grape, and a few cases of those fancy waters. I need everything ASAP. And lemons. And sugar—lots of everything."

"Grace is on her way home from class," John said. "I'll send her."

"Great. Thanks so much." Albert slid the phone back into his jeans' pocket and set out to tackle the mess at his feet.

Fortunately, it took the dinner guests a little time to be seated, then Bishop Atlee's prayer was a long one. Grace arrived in less time than Albert would have thought possible, and he started squeezing lemons while she directed those women serving to carry trays of sodas and flavored water to the guests.

By three in the afternoon Grace was able to leave to pick up 'Kota from school, and shortly thereafter, Albert was on his way. Smiling to himself, he drove out of the yard. In a few hours, he'd be back to share another meal with Hannah, the bridal party, and their family, friends and neighbors. It wouldn't be soon enough to suit Albert, because in all the commotion, he'd missed his lunch again. Still, he felt good as he pulled onto the blacktop at the end of Hannah's lane.

The only thing that troubled him was wondering what to do about Susanna. Telling on her would mean upset for Hannah and for Susanna, but not telling might lead to bigger problems. The fact of the matter was, Hannah had a serious problem. Susanna wasn't like other girls her age. She was innocent in so many ways, but she was a grown woman in others. First Susanna was sneaking out in the middle of the night to be with a boy. Now she was kissing a boy. It was his duty to tell her mother what he'd seen, wasn't it?

Albert rubbed his chin and realized that it was bristly.

"First thing I have to do is shower and shave," he murmured aloud. "That and have a good talk with the Lord." Sometimes, life threw questions at a man he couldn't answer. And then the best thing—the only thing—to do was to take it to the Almighty in prayer.

# Chapter Ten

❧

At eight-fifteen the following morning Hannah walked out onto the back porch, saw Albert's truck parked by the stable door, and went to find him. She hadn't gotten to bed until late the previous night, but she'd slept in until six-thirty, which was a luxury. Usually, in spring and summer, she was up before the sun. The nice thing was that the house was absolutely quiet this morning, something she'd rarely experienced in all the years it had been her home.

Hannah's houseguest, Sara, had walked across the field to have breakfast with Lydia Byler. Susanna had left after the wedding supper with her sister Anna to sleep over, and Irwin was fishing today. As for the newlyweds, contrary to the usual custom of spending their wedding night at the bride's parents', they'd chosen to bundle Caleb's small, sleepy daughter into their buggy and return to their own home shortly after nine the previous night.

Tired but pleased by how well Rebecca's wedding had gone, Hannah couldn't help feeling a little guilty by how relieved she was that she'd found good husbands for all of her marriageable daughters. It had been her prayer for so many years. Now it had been fulfilled. But the niggling worry over Susanna was still there.

Hannah had kept an eye on her at the reception and later at the supper and the barn games that followed that the young people so enjoyed. Susanna had seemed to enjoy herself as much as anyone, but she and David King had barely glanced at one another. Was it too much to hope that they had grown bored with each other's company? So, life was good this morning, and she had much to be thankful for.

Albert Hartman was one of those blessings, and she wanted to thank him for his help the previous day. She didn't know why she'd panicked at so small a thing as an upset drink table, but at the time, it had seemed like a disaster. Mercifully, Albert had been there to take over. When she'd gone into the kitchen, she'd found him and Grace happily squeezing bags of lemons. Albert had heated the lemon juice and stirred in the sugar before pouring the mixture over blocks of ice, creating the best lemonade Hannah had ever tasted.

And he'd brought bottles of fruit juice and the other drinks. There had been so much left over, even after supper, that she'd have plenty to take to church and share on the next worship Sunday. She had thanked him last night when he had left with his family, but she wanted to thank him again. He really had gone beyond what most would have done. Especially with him being male. Hannah didn't know a single man in her family who would have taken on the job so good-naturedly or with such success.

Hannah found Albert cleaning out the alpacas' water trough in the loafing shed. A circle of alpacas stood motionless a few yards away, ears perked and wide-eyed, watching his every movement. Every time Hannah looked at the animals, she wanted to laugh. They didn't look real; they were more like children's stuffed toys.

She had learned from Albert that alpacas were domesticated animals from the camel family, and originated in South America. They looked like llamas, but were smaller and cuter, in Hannah's opinion, with fluffy heads and bodies. They came in colors ranging from white to very dark brown and Albert's herd represented a variety of colors.

"Good morning!" Hannah called as she stepped through the doorway of the stable. At the sound of her voice, one of the alpaca females whirled around and trotted out into the pasture, followed by all the rest. "Sorry," Hannah said, watching them go. "Didn't mean to frighten them away."

Albert stood and wiped his wet hands on his pant legs. He looked especially nice this morning. He was freshly shaven and his hair, which had recently been cut, was neatly combed. He was wearing a new long-sleeved chambray shirt over tan twill trousers and leather boots. He had rolled up his sleeves, and Hannah couldn't help noticing how muscular his arms were.

*Not proper thoughts for a respectable widow,* she mentally chided herself. Unfortunately, although she could control her speech, there was little she could do about her sometimes wayward thoughts. She was approaching fifty, but she wasn't blind or in her grave.

"Don't worry about it." He smiled at her in a way that warmed her heart. "I think it's a game they play. I doubt they're nearly as frightened of us as they pretend to be."

"I think they can be brave if they need to be," Hannah agreed. "My friend said that her herd regularly chases coyotes away from the livestock. Some of her neighbors are buying alpacas instead of guard dogs."

"Maybe we should tell Tim Fisher. He lost two lambs to stray dogs last month." Albert opened the valve that would let water into the trough. The windmill pumped fresh water from the well to the house as well as to the barns. He folded his arms and leaned back against an upright post. "It was a nice wedding supper, Hannah. I ate so much, I don't think I'll eat again for a week." He patted his abdomen.

She chuckled. She liked the idea of providing Albert with good, home-cooked meals. Every man who worked as hard as he did deserved to be well fed. "I doubt that. I know what an appetite you have."

He grimaced in mock shame and glanced down at the ground. "Guilty as charged."

"I wanted to thank you for yesterday—for the drinks—the lemonade especially. You're a good friend."

He stepped away from the post and his posture stiffened. "I like to think so."

Albert's forehead creased and his expression grew serious, making Hannah think that there was something more he wanted to say and was finding it difficult.

"I mean it, Albert. I don't know what I would have done about replacing the drinks without delaying dinner and risking the food getting cold. I know it's prideful, but I'd have been embarrassed to serve nothing more than water."

He held up his hand. "Say no more about it. You would have made do, Hannah. I have every confidence that no one would have gone thirsty at your table."

She smiled, secretly pleased at his praise. "Thank you."

He glanced at the ground, then back up at her. "You may not be thanking me when I tell you what I saw yesterday. It's not my place to interfere in your family, but..." He hesitated.

She didn't like the look on his face. It was something awful. She could see that.

He closed the distance between them, his gaze meeting hers. "Hannah, the table with the drinks didn't just fall on its own," he said quietly. "I'm sure the one leg wasn't properly locked in place, as I mentioned before, but it fell because David and Susanna backed into it." He seemed to hold his breath. "They were kissing, Hannah. I came around the corner and surprised them. Kissing."

She caught the corner of her apron and clasped it tightly in her fist. "Kissing?" She thought for a moment, glancing at the ground, then back at him. There had been a minor kissing incident with Susanna and David before, but she thought she had nipped that in the bud. "Like, on the cheek?"

"No," he answered firmly. She saw his face redden. "More like kissing-kissing. A little awkward, but it definitely wasn't the first time for either of them."

"Oh, my." Hannah's knees felt weak. With a

sharp inhale, she sank onto a bale of straw that stood by the shed door. "This is a bad thing, Albert." She shook her head. "A really bad thing."

"I'm sorry to be the bearer of bad news. I didn't want to trouble you with it yesterday. I wondered if it was my place to tell you, at all." He hesitated. "But, Hannah, if Susanna was my daughter and you had seen what I saw, I would have wanted you to tell me."

She looked up at him. "*Ne,* thank you. You were right to come to me with this." She shook her head again. "I'm such a fool. I thought maybe, *hoped* she had gotten over him." She lifted her hands and let them fall into her lap. "But obviously she hasn't."

"Is it such a terrible thing, Hannah?" He was standing close, his eyes clouded with compassion. "Kissing a boy?"

Hannah clasped her hands tightly. "There *is* a place for kissing, Albert. That place is in marriage. For Susanna and David to behave like a married couple is inappropriate." She pressed her hand to her forehead. "Not to mention dangerous." She glanced up at him. "You and I both know what other behavior it could lead to."

"She's a good girl."

"*Ya,* Susanna is a good girl, but her judgment isn't sound. Grace's 'Kota is a good boy, but you wouldn't hand him the keys to your truck and let him drive down Route 13. He's not ready for such responsibility any more than Susanna is ready to play flirting games with boys."

He was quiet for a minute, letting her think, which she appreciated. It didn't feel awkward, the silence between them. It was comforting to Hannah to have his opinion and offer hers. It had been a long time since she'd been able to talk to a man this way. Not since Jonas.

"What will you do about it?" Albert finally asked, taking a seat beside her on the bale. He was close, but not so close that his clothing or a knee or elbow touched hers.

"I don't know. I honestly don't know." She looked at her hands in her lap. "I'll speak to the two of them, of course. And David's parents must be told." Her throat felt scratchy as if she were about to burst into tears, but she wouldn't give in to emotion. "It can't happen again."

"Do you think this is happening because you've tried to keep them apart?" Albert asked hesitantly.

"I haven't been trying to keep them apart." She was quiet for a second. "Not really."

"Do *they* think you're trying to keep them apart?" He asked, then went on. "Have you considered that Susanna may know her own heart? What if she and David really are in love?"

Hannah frowned. "Susanna is too immature to understand that kind of love." She shook off his argument like stray raindrops. "I know my own child."

"Maybe," he answered, his voice gentle. "But what if Susanna isn't a child anymore?"

As she crossed the field to Anna and Samuel's farmhouse, the clouds overhead thickened and Hannah heard the rumble of thunder in the distance. She wondered if she should have taken the time to hitch the horse up to the buggy, but Anna's home was so close and David's parents not much farther in the opposite direction. It had seemed a waste. Besides, even if she did get wet, walking would ease some of her pent-up tension.

She couldn't get Albert's words out of her head. *What if Susanna isn't a child anymore?*

He was wrong, of course; he didn't know her well enough to understand. He only saw Susanna occasionally, in specific circumstances. Anyone who lived with her day in and day out would understand how unprepared she was for the responsibility of marriage, for running a household. Anyone who knew her as Hannah did would know she didn't understand the feelings that could exist between a man and a woman.

But doubt nudged at Hannah's conscience. What if her judgment was clouded by a mother's desire to protect her special-needs child? What if

Albert was right and she was the one who wasn't seeing the situation clearly?

Hannah didn't know what to do with that notion, so for practicality's sake, she pushed it aside.

She would collect her wayward daughter, the daughter who'd been so well-behaved yesterday, at least when her mother was watching. And they would talk about what Albert had witnessed. Together, they would go to David's and speak with him and his parents. Somehow, they had to find a solution—a solution that didn't involve any more illicit kissing.

"Oh, Susanna," she fretted aloud.

Susanna and David knew better. Their parents had taught them better. Their community had rules and standards, and a member had to abide by those conventions or risk censuring, even shunning.

Hannah walked faster, pumping her arms, her bonnet strings flying behind her. The problem was that Susanna could be so obstinate. And something told her that her daughter had already made up her mind about David. So how in the name of decency was she going to stop Susanna's inappropriate behavior?

Late that afternoon, as rain pelted the windows and drummed on the porch roof, Hannah sat drinking herbal tea at her own kitchen table with her friend Sara. A chastened Susanna had come home, spent an hour in her library, and then hurried upstairs to her bedroom. David, when Hannah had last seen him, had been shoveling out his mother's chicken house. He might still be at the task for all she knew.

"Sara, how could I have been so foolish?" Hannah asked. She felt as limp and powerless as a wet dishtowel when it was wrung out and hung up to dry. "To let it go on under my own nose—to not put two and two together?" She'd told Sara the whole unpleasant story, not about just the kissing, but the incident with the pony cart, and Susanna's recent rebellions and sullen stubbornness.

Although many miles separated them, Hannah had always considered Sara one of her dearest friends. They were close in age and both widowed. Through letters, phone calls and occasional visits, the two had remained close over the years. Sara was the kind of friend that, when they did come face-to-face, it was as if they had left off talking the day before. Sara was sensible and plain-spoken. Hannah didn't have to tiptoe around her, and she knew that any advice offered would be sound.

Sara nodded sympathetically and poured more tea from a pretty blue-and-white porcelain teapot. Sara preferred tea to coffee, and Hannah had made certain she had a good supply of her friend's favorites in the cupboard before her arrival.

"Did they try to deny what they'd been up to?" Sara asked, her plump, red-brown face shiny with concern. "Or did they own up to the mischief?" Her sloe-black eyes narrowed shrewdly.

Hannah grimaced. "Susanna tried to pretend she had no idea what I was talking about, but David turned red as a pickled beet and started to cry."

"What did his parents say?"

"They were shocked, naturally. Ebben, David's father, was angry. Apparently, David's never been a problem for them, not until my daughter came along, at least. Lately, there's been some misbehavior in their household, too. Apparently, David's been here without permission several times. Times when he led us to believe that his parents were aware of where he was. The two of them, Susanna and David, have been misleading us all."

"Young people," Sara said kindly. "It happens."

Hannah sighed audibly, her heart going out to Sadie and Ebben. "It can't be easy for them. They're new to our community, and trouble is the last thing they want." Hannah raised her cup to her lips and then put it back in the saucer untouched. She hesitated before speaking again. "Do you know what Sadie said?" Sara was listening intently; Hannah went on, "That we should consider letting them walk out together. Like any boy and girl. With proper courting rules."

"So," Sara pursed her lips. "What do you think of that?"

Hannah met her friend's penetrating gaze. "I didn't want to hurt their feelings, so I said I would think on the matter, but the idea is...it's impossible."

"Why impossible?" Sara broke off a piece of gingerbread and popped it into her mouth.

"To what end?" Hannah opened her arms and let her hands rest on the table again. "You know Susanna. And you've met David. There can be no real courting between them. Courting is done with the intention of marriage."

Sara slowly chewed her gingerbread and sipped her tea.

"You think I'm being overprotective." It was a statement, not a question. Hannah swallowed. The gingerbread smelled delicious, but she couldn't eat a bite. Her stomach was still doing flip-flops. "I've always tried to treat Susanna the same as her sisters, but she *isn't* the same. There's so much about the world that she doesn't understand. That she'll never understand."

"It's a natural thing for young women to be attracted to men," Sara said. "And Susanna has watched every one of her sisters court and marry.

Why wouldn't she think the same opportunity is available to her?"

"Because I've told her it isn't," Hannah said, firmly.

"And did that work?" Sara smiled and went on. "We can't help how we feel, Hannah. And God meant us to marry. Each and every one of us."

"You think marriage is the answer to everything." Their gazes met again, and Hannah realized how harsh that must have sounded to her friend. "I'm sorry, Sara. I didn't mean to snap at you." She pressed her lips tightly together, truly unsure as to what to do. It was times like this that she so missed the companionship of a husband. This had been so much easier when there had been two of them to make these kinds of decisions. "What do I do?" she asked softly. "I don't know how to protect Susanna, but still do what's right."

Sara didn't answer right away. Instead, she let Hannah's question hang in the air. She bit off another piece of gingerbread, chewed slowly and sipped more tea. "Maybe you should consider the Kings' suggestion," she said after several minutes passed. "Because, you know how stubborn Susanna can be. And frankly, short of locking her in the attic or sending her to Brazil, how *would* you keep them apart?"

Hannah shrugged. "Sadie thinks that might be

the root of all the sneaking around." Albert had said the same thing, but she didn't bring that up. "The more Sadie's tried to steer David away from Susanna, the more insistent he's become."

Hannah fiddled with her teaspoon. "It's all my fault. When David first came to Seven Poplars, I encouraged the friendship. I wanted Susanna to have a companion like her. I knew she was lonely, I—" She shook her head. "It never occurred to me that this could happen."

Sara sliced another sliver of gingerbread from the serving plate.

"Maybe Sadie's right. Maybe we've driven them to this." Hannah added more sugar to her tea. "But is letting them go to singings and young people's frolics really a solution?"

"I think it's an idea worth considering. If they were officially courting, the whole community would be chaperoning them. It's the way things are done for a reason, Hannah." Sara rose from the table and walked to the rocking chair where her Molly was curled up on an old blanket. Sara stroked the dog's head and rubbed her silky ears.

Hannah sighed. "Maybe you're right. I don't know. I just don't know."

"Then you must pray for an answer," Sara said. "I find that most problems are settled by prayer." She smiled. Her teeth were very white and even. Sara had a lovely smile. It was one of her best features. "He has a plan for each of us, although sometimes, it may seem to us that the path is rocky or muddy. We must have faith, Hannah."

"I try." Hannah took a sip of the tea and made a face. "But I have to admit, I find this tea bitter."

Sara laughed. "So, I'll make you some coffee. I'm not offended. To each her own. But I think we're a lot more alike than different. We are both accustomed to getting our way, and it's hard to give up control, even to a higher power."

"Or in this case, a wayward daughter." Hannah smiled back at Sara and reached for the gingerbread. She'd have a small piece. She hadn't eaten anything since breakfast. Maybe going without her midday meal was what had made her so jittery. "I'm so glad you're here," she said, purposely changing the subject. "Just thinking about the possibility of having you for a neighbor, it would be wonderful, Sara. Wisconsin is so far away."

"I have to say, I like your community and having you nearby would make settling in so much easier. The longer I'm in Seven Poplars, the more I think the Lord might be calling me here." She adjusted her white *kapp,* almost identical to Hannah's. "I've never gotten used to the Wisconsin winters. We had snow up to my shoulders in February and temperatures of thirty below."

"Brrr. I can't imagine." Hannah got up to make

a pot of coffee. "You may want to have a look at the property next to Caleb and Rebecca's. The house is one story with modern appliances. It was an English house, so you'd need to have the electricity removed, but Caleb says the stove and water heater are propane. There's a pellet stove that heats most of the house, which would work for you."

"How much land?"

"Seven acres, maybe a little less, but there are some outbuildings. The garage might do for your horse and buggy. And there's another house on our road. It's about a half mile from here, on the right. It has less land, but the house is—" A knock at the kitchen door drew her attention. She crossed the room and glanced through the window. "Oh, it's Albert." She opened the door. "Albert, hello, come in."

He stepped into the kitchen, his dark green rain slicker dripping, saw Sara and stopped short. "Sorry, Hannah, I didn't mean to interrupt." He tugged off his ball cap. "Hello, Sara."

She nodded. "Albert."

"How's Molly doing?"

"Much better today," Sara said. "As you said, a few days of rest and she'll be her old self."

"I didn't mean to intrude." Albert looked to Hannah, his face reddening. "I was feeding... I was wondering how you... I knew that you were upset about Susanna," he continued as he backed out onto the porch. "I just wanted to see if you were…"

Hannah followed him onto the porch. Rain fell, making it seem later than five o'clock. Still, it was time she got an evening meal together. "Thank you, Albert. It's kind of you to be concerned for me and my family."

He retreated down the steps to the yard. "It'll be all right. With Susanna. You're a good mother, Hannah. The best. Susanna will be fine."

She thanked him again and returned to the kitchen. Sara had returned to her place at the table and had picked up her knitting bag. She was working on a small navy mitten.

"Albert is the one who caught Susanna and David kissing," Hannah explained.

Sara raised one dark eyebrow quizzically. "So you told me."

"He's a good friend," Hannah added.

"I can tell." She cut her dark eyes at Hannah. "Are you and Albert courting?"

"Courting?" Hannah's eyes widened with surprise. "*Courting?* Of course, not. I told you, he's a friend. He…he comes by so often because… Well, to look after the alpacas."

"Mmm-hmm." Sara studied her. "But I see the way he looks at you. Whatever you feel for this man, he considers you more than a friend."

"That can't be," Hannah protested, her thoughts immediately racing back to the restaurant, where Albert had taken her hand. And how she had felt when he touched her. She knew her face was turning red. She could feel the heat. "*Ne.* You're mistaken, Sara—" She was so flustered that she was having a hard time finding her tongue. She turned to the sink, embarrassed. "He…he's not Plain. It would never—"

"You were once Mennonite, weren't you?"

"*Ya,* but I could never…" She let her sentence trail off as she slowly turned to face her friend again.

"Maybe you could and maybe you couldn't," Sara replied, shrugging her broad shoulders, "but men and women, that's one thing I understand." She scrutinized Hannah with her dark eyes. "I'm glad you brought this up, because I wanted to talk to you about your situation. You've been alone too long. Whether it be Albert Hartman or someone else, it's high time you married."

## Chapter Eleven

All Hannah could do for a moment was shake her head. *"Ne, ne,"* she stammered. "You must have misunderstood. Albert doesn't—"

*"Mam!"* Susanna pounded down the staircase. *"Mam,* there's a van." She skipped past Hannah and Sara to the window. "Look!" She pointed. "It a blue van."

Sara got to her feet. "It's about time. I expected them an hour ago."

Hannah joined Susanna at the window. Through the rain, she could see an English man come around the vehicle.

Hannah glanced back at Sara and nodded. *"Ya,* this must be your Ellie," she said as she went out onto the porch. Susanna and Sara followed.

"Is this the Yoder place?" the man called.

*"Ya!"* Sara answered. "You're at the right house."

They watched as he opened the sliding door

of the van, removed a white plastic stool and set it in on the driveway. The driver went around to the back of the van and lifted out a black suitcase, then hurried back to the sliding door where he opened a big black umbrella.

A small figure in a black Amish bonnet, white prayer *kapp* and black cape stepped down onto the stepstool and then onto the ground. She waved toward the house. "Sara! I'm here! I made it."

Sara laughed and waved Ellie in. "Don't be shy, girl. Come and get in out of the rain."

Ellie laughed and trudged across the muddy yard toward the porch steps, trying to stay under the umbrella the man carried.

"She's a *kinder,*" Susanna exclaimed, clapping her hands.

*"Ne,"* Sara corrected gently. "Ellie is not a child. She's twenty-three, a year older than you."

"Ellie is a little person," Hannah explained. She gave Susanna a look and put her finger to her lips. "I expect you to be on your best behavior and make her welcome in our home."

"I will, *Mam,*" Susanna promised. A wide smile split her face. "She can sleep in my room."

At the steps, the man slid the suitcase onto the porch and handed Ellie the umbrella. They exchanged a few words, then he tipped his hat to the women on the porch and hurried back across the wet yard to his van.

"*Wilkom,* Ellie," Sara said. "We wondered when you'd get here. How was your trip?" She took the black suitcase. "And your mother?"

"*Gut, gut,*" Ellie replied with a dimpled smile as she took the porch steps, one at a time. "We got a late start from the Shetlers' because the van wouldn't start. He called AAA and an Englisher garage man came, but he didn't have a new battery. Andy Shetler told him he should have had a mule because they don't need batteries." She chuckled as she folded her umbrella and leaned it against the outside kitchen wall. "We got here to Kent County and then the driver had some trouble finding Leroy Hostetler's to drop off their cousins, but finding you was easy after that."

Hannah returned the smile. She liked the cheerful blue-eyed girl at once. "All that way you came. Sara said you live near her in Wisconsin."

"*Ya,*" Ellie replied as they trooped into the kitchen. "But I came just from Pennsylvania today. The driver's already headed back to Wisconsin, picking up a family in Ohio on his way."

"We'll have supper in just a bit," Hannah said, after introductions and greetings were exchanged all around. "But first I think you'd best get into some dry things." She motioned to Susanna. "Can you take our guest to her room show her where to put her belongings?"

"*Ya,*" Ellie agreed as she pushed a dripping

lock of hair off her forehead. "I do need to *rett up* a bit before I'm fit for your kitchen."

Susanna nodded shyly.

"Will you be my first new friend in Delaware?" Ellie asked her.

*"Ya."* Susanna nodded. "I will be your friend. Come on!" Grinning, she led Ellie away toward the back of the house.

"She's lovely," Hannah said to Sara. "But are you certain that…"

"She'll find a good match, being so small?" Sara brushed a wrinkle out of her apron. "Just wait and see."


Albert had lured Nina over to the side of the stall with bits of carrot and was now stroking her back. She was turning out to be the friendliest of the herd, so far. Or at least the bravest. "Do you like that, girl?" he asked. The feel of the fleece, so soft and thick, never failed to amaze him. His love of animals had been a passion in his life since he was a young child, but the joy these alpacas gave him was a thrill of which he never tired. It was so peaceful here in Hannah's barn with the rain drumming on the roof. Albert suspected he should have felt guilty for leaving work early—something he rarely allowed himself, but he didn't. Here in the peace of the barn, he could feel the tension of the day's stress draining out of him.

Abruptly, Nina raised her head and stared past Albert. At almost the same instant, he became aware of the soft tread of footsteps. The alpaca flicked her ears, wrinkled her nose and retreated a few steps, just out of reach.

"Albert?" It was Hannah's friend, Sara.

"Yes," he answered, turning to face her. He couldn't imagine why she would seek him out. "Molly's okay, isn't she?"

Sara nodded. "*Ya,* all is well with her. I saw your truck was still here and I wanted to speak with you." Her tone was frank, not abrasive, but more direct than that of most Amish women with whom he came in contact.

He regarded her with curiosity.

"You and my cousin Hannah are friends, *ya?*" she asked.

Albert slid his thumbs into his pants pockets and nodded. "We are."

She took a step closer. She was plump and no taller than five-one or five-two, but she had a way of commanding the space around her. This woman was a force to be reckoned with.

"Are you a man of faith, Albert Hartman?" she asked.

Albert blinked. *Faith?* He nodded again. "Yes, I think I am." Where was Sara going with this?

*"Gut."* She smiled at him with an expression of approval that lit her strong, plain face with an inner light. "And are you are a single man who is unmarried and has given no pledge to any woman?"

"Sara, I don't—"

She cut him off. *"Ne,* Albert. Hear me out." She slipped into the *Deitsch* dialect that he understood perfectly. "It is clear to me that you are very fond of our Hannah."

"Of course, I am." He glanced nervously away, and then back at her. "I have the greatest respect for Hannah."

Tiny lines crinkled at the corners of Sara's dark eyes. "How deep does this *fondness* go?"

"I…I'm not sure how to answer that question."

"Albert, do you know what I do?" Sara chuckled and rested her fists against ample hips. "How I make my living?"

"I don't. Hannah mentioned that you were widowed. I suppose I assumed—"

"That my husband left me well provided for?" She shrugged and made a gesture with both hands that could have been amusement or complete agreement.

Again, Albert found himself perplexed by this unusual visitor that seemed so similar to all the Amish women he'd known, and yet not, with her very non-German features and her deep honey-brown skin. "I suppose I did," he answered.

"I am twice-widowed," she said. "And both my late husbands were blessed with substantial material possessions. But I have always been a woman who wanted to maintain a state of independence, and so I have my own trade." She chuckled and Albert saw that her teeth were white and even. "I am a matchmaker, Albert," she explained. "I specialize in arranging marriages among the Amish." Sara searched for the right way to continue. "For those women who, for whatever reason, have found it difficult to make their own matches."

"A marriage broker?" He could hardly believe it. An Amish matchmaker? He'd never heard of such a thing. It was true that most Old Order Amish women married, regardless of looks or disposition. But it had never occurred to him that such a service existed.

"*Ya,* it is what I do, and God has seen it to bless my efforts. No case is too difficult if my clients are willing to listen to reason. Naturally, you wouldn't know of my work or others like me. What I do is private, though well respected. It is a profession that stretches back centuries, to the Old World of Austria and Switzerland. But it isn't a tradition we care to share with the Englishers. Too often, they like to seize on every aspect of our private lives and call us quaint and old-fashioned."

Albert got the impression he was just supposed to listen, but not respond.

"You may know of one match I arranged. Aunt Jezzy, Hannah's mother-in-law's sister."

"Yes, I know Jezzy, but I thought—"

Again, Sara chuckled. "You think that a woman of Jezzy's age and shy nature would suddenly meet and be swept off her feet by an equally shy man who just happened to live nine miles away?" She folded her arms over her bosom. "A very good match, if I do say so myself."

He couldn't imagine where this was going. "You're telling me that you are paid to bring couples together, sort of like a horse-and-buggy dating service?"

Sara pursed her lips. "Not dating, Albert, *matchmaking.* I make marriages for people, solid marriages."

"But what does this have to do with me?" he blurted.

"Exactly what I was getting to. I need to know your intentions." Sara's dark, piercing eyes locked with his. "Speak up," she insisted, though she really hadn't given him the time to respond. "There can be no shyness between us if this is to work. Now, be honest with me. How deeply does this fondness for Hannah Yoder run? Could you see yourself as her husband?"

For a moment he was so astounded by what

she said that he couldn't find his voice. "I—I'm Mennonite. She's Amish." He shook his head. "I assumed…" He met her gaze. "Surely, that would be impossible, wouldn't it?"

"Please answer the question," she said. "A simple *ya* or *ne* will do. Could you see the two of you as man and wife?"

He took a step backward. Wiped his mouth with his hand. "Maybe." He looked at his boots, suddenly as uncomfortable as he had ever been in his life. He knew his face had to be bright red. "I…I'm not sure," he mumbled. "I…I care for Hannah, but the differences in our faiths make it—"

"Albert Hartman. No wonder you've never married. You look for the negative rather than the positive. It is rare for people to meet someone who touches their heart. You and Hannah obviously have."

He lifted his gaze from his boots to Sara's face. His heart was now pounding. "Hannah would never—"

"Tish!" Sara gave a sound of impatience. "Didn't you just tell me that you were a man of faith?"

"Yes, but…" He grimaced. "Why are we having this conversation? I don't even know if she likes me *that* way. She and I have never discussed courting."

"Exactly my point. You haven't considered the possibility. So you sit there like a stump, enduring your loneliness, living a life that's only half-full when someone like Hannah—who is as lonely as you—longs for the love and companionship that you both deserve." She threw up her arms. "Show that faith you profess. Take a chance on being rejected. What do you have to lose?"

"What are you saying?" he asked, knowing what he thought she meant, but certain he had misunderstood somewhere along the way.

She blinked, shaking her head. "I'm saying, Albert, that you should court Hannah so you can get to know each other. Although from what I gather, you've already been seeing a good deal of each other."

"But how could we ever— I'm a veterinarian. Amish men don't become veterinarians."

"There you go trying to put the cart before the horse again. First see if this is something you both want. If it is, drop to your knees and pray to the Almighty to show you how to accomplish it. You can't surrender without even trying, or can you?"

He stared at the loose straw at his feet. "I have prayed for someone," he admitted. The warmth in his cheeks now seemed to be spreading through his whole body. "I've wondered why it is that other people find someone, but never me."

"Do you believe that the Lord should drag you

to the right woman by the scruff of your neck? Don't you think that He expects you to make an effort?" She made a dismissive sniff. "Make a start here and now. Come to the house and join us at the table. Show Hannah that you are interested in her in an honorable way and see where God's mercy leads you." Sara folded her plump arms. "Of course, she may reject you as she has rejected other suitors, but you'll never know unless you try."

"What if *I'm* not certain?"

"Then standing here will never help you to make up your mind. Fear, Albert. You've let fear and doubt rule your mind. You and Hannah must take a good look at each other."

"I can't just invite myself to her table," he protested weakly. Even as he spoke the words, he knew he would come. He couldn't not come if there was a chance that Sara was right—that there might be a way that he and Hannah could be together, if she cared for him as much as he cared for her.

Sara tilted her head and arched one dark eyebrow. "Oh, you won't be." A smile teased the corners of her mouth. "She sent me out here to ask you to share our meal."

Somehow, Hannah got through supper, although if her life had depended on it, she couldn't

have said what she served or ate. Through the
entire meal, she kept thinking of how foolish it
was that she'd allowed Sara to talk her into in-
viting Albert. Where was her head? It had been
one thing to invite him to eat with them when
he was just a friend of the family, but now that
Sara had come straight out and asked if they were
courting, it seemed entirely different. It *felt* different. Hannah knew she was in over her head.
She was a good swimmer, but she'd never gone
into the ocean during a riptide, and that's what
this felt like.

From grace to dessert she was giddy and
*doplich*. Clumsy. She tried to pour sweet tea for
Albert, missed and soaked his hand and the ivory-
colored tablecloth. Then, carrying a blue-willow
dish of flower-shaped butter pats that had been
leftover from the wedding meal, she'd let the plate
slip though her fingers and crash onto the floor.

Albert, true to form, had helped clean up the
broken china and ruined butter, but she had been
mortified. What must Sara's friend Ellie think of
her? Hannah knew she was behaving as foolish as
a teenager at her first singing with a boy. And she
felt like it inside: excited and scared at the same
time and trying hard not to show it.

As everyone talked and ate, Hannah told herself over and over that she would not, *could not,*
seriously consider Albert as a suitor. So why did

the forbidden thought keep bubbling up? There was no getting around it. She, practical Hannah, mother of eight, nine if you counted Irwin, was suddenly an emotional mess over a man.

Somehow, they all got through supper. Dessert and coffee were served and neither Ellie nor Susanna seemed to notice that anything was amiss. As for Irwin, so long as his plate was full, he wouldn't have noticed if the bishop had ridden a cow into the kitchen with a colander on his head and delivered a sermon. Whatever Albert thought of her capricious behavior, he was too much of a gentleman to let it show.

"Well, I guess I'd best be getting home." Albert got up and carried his plate and silverware to the sink where Hannah was standing. "It was a pleasure meeting you, Ellie. I hope you like Seven Poplars."

"I think I will," she replied. Ellie had already begun to help clear the table as if she were part of the family, further endearing her to Hannah. "Everyone here seems so nice," she added.

Albert slowly turned his gaze to Hannah.

Hannah glanced at the floor, then at the dishcloth in her hand and then at Sara. She wanted to look anywhere but at Albert. She could feel her cheeks growing warm again. *What's wrong with me?* Maybe what she needed was a good dose of peppermint tea. Peppermint was good for calming both a queasy stomach and an agitated mind.

"Hannah."

She started. Albert's voice was unusually firm. "Yes?" she said.

"Could I speak with you? Alone." He glanced at Sara and the others. "It was good seeing everyone. If you'll excuse us."

Hannah didn't know what to say. Her tongue stuck to the roof of her mouth. Her feet were anchored to the floor. She clenched the dishcloth so tightly that water dripped on her apron. He must have noticed there was something wrong at supper. Now he was going to ask. She couldn't very well tell him the truth, and embarrass herself further. Risk embarrassing him. What was she going to say? She slowly let the dishrag fall from her fingertips to land in the sink.

"Hannah, will you walk outside with me?" Albert asked. It was a question, but his tone surprised her. He wasn't really asking so much as telling her.

She left the comfort of the sink and followed him across the kitchen. She allowed him to open the screen door for her and to steady her arm as they went down the porch steps. The rain had stopped, but it was very humid.

"Albert, I…" She… What? What was she going to say to him? How could she explain her flustered behavior? Did she come right out and tell him what Sara had asked? Maybe then they would both laugh together over it and she'd stop feeling so foolish. "Albert, I should…"

"Hannah, don't talk." He seemed to tower over her. Had she noticed how much taller he was than her before this? "Please," he said, "I need you to listen to what I have to say before I lose my nerve."

His words immediately caught her attention. And something about the tone of his voice. She was getting that giddy feeling again.

They were standing by the gatepost, within arm's reach but not touching. She raised her head and looked into his eyes. For an instant, there in the fading twilight, she felt the jolt of his intense gaze. And then, before she could react, she got a face full of raindrops as another shower swept over them in a drenching wave.

Albert grabbed her hand. "Quick!" he said. "Into the truck!" He dashed across the yard, pulling her with him.

Hannah's heart was suddenly pounding. He was holding her hand! She knew that it was wrong, but it was impossible to break free. The wicked truth was, she didn't want to be free. Suddenly having Albert's big hand wrapped firmly around hers was as sweet as the smell of newly baked bread. Laughing, she threw caution to the wind and ran after him. She didn't care about the rain, didn't care if her children and guests were watching, didn't care if she was breaking every rule she'd lived by for more than thirty years.

He was laughing, too, as he flung open the vehicle door, caught her by the waist, and lifted her inside. She scooted over on the seat, and he scrambled up, slamming the door behind him. Rain beat at the windows, shutting them away from the world in a private place.

Hannah's *kapp* was soaked. Her hair dripped onto her wet skin and wetter clothing, but it was a warm summer rain and she was too happy to care. She felt the strength in Albert's broad hand and glanced down to see that his fingers were locked around hers. A strong hand, firm and warm. But a lifetime of modest behavior intervened. "Albert, you shouldn't be… We can't…" She knew she should untangle his grasp, but it felt so good, so safe that she didn't know if she had the strength. "Albert," she began softly, "this isn't proper."

He nodded, both his mouth and eyes smiling. He cleared his throat and his expression turned serious. "We aren't kids."

"*Ne,* we aren't." He hadn't let go. Her heart was still racing, her breath coming in short gasps. Could he feel her trembling? Thunder rumbled nearby, and it grew darker outside the cab. The rain came harder, and their breath was beginning to fog the windows. Hannah was aware of Albert's clean, manly scent, of wet leather boots, the faint smell of shaving cream, and the sweet odors of alpaca feed and timothy hay. She blinked back raindrops in an attempt to clear her vision. Albert filled it.

"I hope you won't be offended, but I...I have to say this," he said. "It's obvious to me that the two of us are attracted to each other." He took a deep breath. Exhaled. "Am I right?"

Hannah was surprised by Albert's forwardness. But maybe a little relieved. This was the chance for her to deny everything, to tell him that he was mistaken, that theirs was a friendship only. But she couldn't. She couldn't lie to Albert and she couldn't lie to herself. It was her turn to take a breath and find her courage. "*Ya,* Albert. I think so."

"You *think* or you *know?*" His eyes narrowed—large, brown, beautiful eyes, eyes that held her and took her breath away. "I don't think I'm imagining things. You care for me, Hannah."

She nodded, pressing her lips together. "I do."

"Good," he pronounced. "Because I care for you, too. A great deal." He hesitated, then went on. "So the question is, what are we going to do about it?"

She tore her gaze from his and murmured, "There's nothing we *can* do."

"We can't jump to that conclusion right away." He squeezed her hand harder, and a sensation of tingling warmth ran up her arm. "I've waited my whole life for someone like you," he said. "And I realized today that now that I've found you, I can't give you up easily. I...I won't."

"I don't know what you're saying."

He rubbed her hand in his with his other hand. "I...I'm not sure, either. I guess what I'm saying is, Hannah Yoder, I'd like permission to walk out with you."

There was a long moment of silence. "I don't know how to answer you," she whispered finally. "I... We don't take courting lightly." Tears suddenly welled in her eyes and she pulled her hand from his. She glanced away, blinking. "Albert, Amish don't date. The purpose of a boy walking out with a girl is to see if they're compatible." A lump rose in her throat. She had to say it. She had to be honest with him. "For marriage."

"I understand that."

Even though they were not holding hands any longer, they were still sitting very closely. Too closely. "You do?"

"What I'm asking is if I can court you with the intention of asking you to be my wife. If we find ourselves compatible," he added. "Which, honestly, I think we already do, but—"

"No," Hannah heard herself say. "No, Albert.

I'm sorry if I gave you the wrong impression." She tried to look out the windshield of his truck, but it was raining too hard for her to see anything. The rain sounded loudly on the roof and the hood of the vehicle. She felt as if it was pounding in her head. "I won't leave my faith, Albert. Not even—" Her voice caught in her throat and she was afraid she was going to embarrass herself by crying outright. She made herself look at him. At his handsome face. "I cannot leave my Amish faith, even for you, Albert. Even though I do…care for you. A great deal."

He slid his hand across the seat toward hers, but stopped an inch from her fingertips. "I thought about that. After Sara came to speak to me about you."

"Sara spoke to you? About me?" she asked, eyes widening with shock. "About *you* and me?"

"She *is* a matchmaker after all," he answered with a little smile. "But anyway, what I was thinking was that I know that you were once Mennonite and became Old Order Amish to marry Jonas. And I know that you can't go back. That you wouldn't. Which means…" He went on faster. "Which means that if you and I decide to get married, I'll have to become Amish. I mean, I want to become Amish. To be with you. To marry you."

Hannah couldn't speak. She was touched, beyond words. And for a moment, she imagined sitting at the supper table with Albert, with her husband, talking about their day. She imagined walking down the hall together toward their bedroom, to sleep in each other's arms. But then reality came back to her. The reality of her life. The Old Order Amish life.

The rain was beginning to let up and she could make out the outline of the barn in the distance. "It's a long process," she argued. "A difficult one. You have to get permission from the bishop. It would have to be discussed by the preachers, the deacon. You have to live as if you were Amish for at least a year." Her thoughts raced. "I don't know what they would think about you being a vet."

"Would they ask me to give up my practice?"

"I don't know," she answered, feeling flustered now. "I suppose accommodations could be made. You could use a driver, maybe. Limit the use of your phone for business only…" Her voice trailed off.

"Faith," he said.

"What?" She looked at him again.

"Faith," he repeated. "I have to have faith. If we're meant to be together, it will happen. That's what Sara told me. And…" He squeezed her hand. "I think you have to have faith as well, Hannah." He held her gaze with his warm brown eyes. "In me and in God."

"Albert," she whispered, sliding her hand just close enough to his so that their fingertips now touched.

"Hannah," he answered. "Let me see what the bishop has to say. Will you give me that?"

How could she say no? How could she give in without even letting him try? At least then, if Bishop Atlee denied his request, then Hannah would know they had tried. She would know she had given Albert—no, her and Albert—a chance.

"Say yes, Hannah."

"I…"

He smiled. "I'll take that as a yes." Then he took her hand, lifted it to his lips and kissed it.

Before she could protest, he released her hand, opened the door of the truck and stepped down. "The rain's stopped for the moment. You should make a run for the house now, while you have the chance."

Numbly, she slid down out of the vehicle. Her skin tingled where Albert had pressed his lips against it. She took one step and then another, away from the truck, away from the man who'd just turned her world upside down. She was giddy, so lighthearted that she wasn't sure she could keep her feet on the ground.

"Have faith," Albert called after her. "I'll find a way. I promise you I will."

She didn't dare look back. If she glanced back,

she might wake and find that it was all a dream, that Albert hadn't just offered to become Amish for her, for them. She stopped and took a deep breath.

*Faith.* He was right. She had to have faith.

A small sound of joy escaped from her throat. If this was God's plan for her, if it truly was… Goose bumps rose on her arms and she hugged herself as she continued on toward the house, suddenly feeling younger than she had in years.

# Chapter Twelve

The following morning, Albert was waiting for John in the employees' parking area at the office. Their other vet hadn't yet arrived, and the only other vehicle there was one of the technicians'. When John pulled in, Albert got out of his truck and walked over to John's window.

"Morning, Uncle Albert," John said with a big smile as he lowered the window. "You're here early. Alpacas all doing well?"

"They're all fine. Just got back from Hannah's. Sit there a moment. I'd like to talk to you." Albert walked around John's truck and slid into the front seat beside him. "I need some advice from you, for a change."

"Sounds serious." John's expression became somber.

"It is. I'm moving toward a decision." Albert

took a deep breath. "And it could affect you and the clinic."

"You're aren't sick, are you?"

"Oh, no," Albert assured him. "Nothing like that. Fit as a fiddle." He put a hand on his nephew's shoulder. "I know you think that I haven't been myself since Dad died and you've been worried about me."

"We all miss Gramps."

"He was the best father any man could have, even more remarkable when you think that his own dad died when he was ten." He wanted to talk to John about Hannah. About everything. He just didn't know how he was going to get there. "Did you know that my grandparents on both sides were Amish? My father left the Amish and later married your grandmother, who'd also left her order. They then became Mennonite."

"I had heard that we had Amish in our family. Gramps didn't talk a lot about his childhood." John rested his hand on the steering wheel. Waited.

"I've been thinking for a long time about my spiritual roots, John. Reading my Bible, praying." Albert gazed out the windshield, then returned his attention to John. "I'm going to ask to join the Amish church."

John's eyes widened. "Because of Hannah?"

It was Albert's turn to be surprised. "Have we... Have I been that obvious?"

John shook his head and smiled. "No, of course not. But Grace and I were talking about this just last night. I'd have to be blind not to see that you're attracted to her, but to change your faith." He glanced out the window, then back at Albert. "Are you sure that this is what you want?"

"If there's any future for me with Hannah, it would have to be that. She could never give up her church."

"But you would yours?" John asked.

Albert thought for a moment before answering. It was good that he was talking to John about this. He knew he could count on his nephew, to be sure Albert was asking himself the right questions. "The way I look at it," he said slowly, "I wouldn't be leaving my faith so much as going back to my grandparents' faith."

John nodded. "And it's what you want? You're willing to give up driving? Electricity?" He hesitated. "What if they wouldn't want you to continue to be a vet?"

"Hannah and I talked about that and I understand that it's a possibility," he said slowly. "And that's why I wanted to talk to you. Because obviously, this could affect you and our practice. I think we could work something out, but if not..." He stopped and started again. "The thing is, I'm willing to take that chance because none of what the world has to offer seems as important as what I've found on Hannah's farm. Family, peace, a feeling of living close to the land and close to God." His voice grew husky. "Finally finding the one woman I want to spend the rest of my life with."

"And she feels the same way?"

He thought before he spoke. "I believe she does, or at least, she could. Do you have any objections to me marrying Hannah? Because if you do, I need to hear them now."

John shook his head. "No, of course not. She's Grace's mother, or as good as. I can't think of any woman I have more respect for, other than my wife." He paused for a moment, then went on. "But, aren't you rushing into things? The two of you have never been out on a date and now you're talking about marrying?

"Your impulsiveness concerns me. It isn't like you. As long as I can remember, you're the one who has been advising me to take my time to make important decisions."

Albert smiled, folded his arms and settled back against the door. "Ordinarily, I'd agree with you. You're right. A man shouldn't rush into a life-changing decision, but you have to remember that I've known Hannah for years, first as a client and the wife of my friend, and then as a widow struggling to run her farm and raise her girls. I've eaten at Hannah's table more times than I can remember. I've gone to family weddings, community frolics and funerals. I never tire of talking to her, and just seeing her always brings a smile to my face." He was quiet for a moment. "Actually, I believe Hannah is the reason that I haven't married anyone else. I've gone out with some nice women, but in my mind, they never quite measured up to Hannah. So it's more than compatibility, John. To be honest, I think I'm in love with her."

"You think you love her?" he repeated.

"I've never felt this way about anyone before. Being with Hannah…well, it makes me feel complete. And if we walk out with each other for a few months, or longer, we can both be certain before we make lifetime vows."

"It sounds as if you're pretty certain that this is what you want," John admitted. "But what you're suggesting, to turn Amish, it won't be easy."

"I know that. It's why I've come to ask for your help." He glanced sheepishly at his nephew. "I was hoping you'd go talk to Samuel with me. I know he's just a deacon, but I think he's a good place to start. We know him a lot better than Bishop Atlee or the new preacher. Hannah's brother-in-law, Reuben Coblentz, him I know well enough, but I'm not sure he'll be all that keen on letting me into the church."

"Not if his wife, Martha, has anything to say about it," John agreed. "When do you want to talk to Samuel?"

"Soon. Hannah and I have already discussed the matter. I want to start spending time with her, and we aren't going to sneak around like teenagers. I'm willing to follow the rules, but I want to get started. Or know it's not a possibility."

"So you and Hannah just discussed this? Recently?"

"Yesterday," Albert answered.

"Well, my advice would be to think on it a few days. Let's make plans to go see Samuel at the end of the week."

"All right." Albert tapped the dashboard. "I'm not going to change my mind, but I can see why you'd say that." He grinned. "I'd likely tell you the same thing."

John ran his hand along the top of the steering wheel. "A year is what I've heard, a year living like one of them, attending church, adopting the clothing. It's to give you the opportunity to see if it's the right path for you and for them."

"Seems fair and reasonable," Albert mused.

Both men were quiet for a moment, lost in their own thoughts. Then Albert smiled wryly at John. "My chances aren't good that things will turn out the way I want them to, are they?"

"Maybe not," John agreed. "But remember

what advice you gave me when I came to you about Grace. You told me to have faith. So, I'll tell you the same thing. Put your trust in God and plunge ahead. 'Faint heart never won fair *frau*.'"

Carrying a split-oak basket, Hannah walked barefoot across the thick, green grass to the garden gate. It was the kind of day that made her want to be outdoors. It was quiet in the garden, with no sound but the chatter of a Carolina wren and the buzz of honey bees. Johanna had taken most of her beehives to her new home on Roland's farm, but she'd left two colonies behind. The bees insured good pollination both in the garden and in the fields, and Hannah loved to see them flitting from blossom to blossom gathering pollen. There was something about bees that just felt right and good to her.

Susanna was busy polishing the stairway banister and woodwork in the parlor. Sara and Ellie had borrowed her horse Blackie and a buggy to meet a prospective bridegroom, and Irwin was working at the chair shop today. Here in her beloved garden, Hannah could find plenty to do, and she would have the peace and solitude to think about all that had happened in the past few days: Rebecca's wedding, her friend Sara's prospective move to Seven Poplars and, most of all, Albert.

Hannah entered the garden and latched the gate

behind her, shutting out any stray sheep or wandering chickens. She suspected that her late strawberries were ripening, and she had a notion to bake a shortcake for the midday meal. Here and there, a few weeds sprouted between the rows of corn, string beans, tomatoes and peppers. Once she'd picked her berries, she'd have to fetch the hoe and see to those intruders. Since Johanna, Anna and Rebecca had left, it was harder to keep the kitchen garden free of weeds, but she had to be vigilant. Left to run wild, they'd choke out her vegetables and leave them without enough food to can for winter.

The warm earth felt good under her bare feet. It never bothered Hannah to drop to her knees when she was picking beans, or in this case, strawberries. Just as she'd thought, there were dozens and dozens at the perfect point of ripeness. She lowered her basket to the ground beside her and began to pluck the scarlet berries. The best thing about working in the garden was that once she'd decided what needed doing, her hands knew the chore, and her mind was free to wander where it would.

Who was she kidding? There would be no wandering.

*Albert.* He was what she wanted to think about! Hannah couldn't help giggling at her own foolishness. She had lain awake until the clock struck two last night, then slept late and had been disappointed to discover, when she got to the barn, that Albert had already been there to take care of the alpacas and gone. She'd so badly wanted to see him this morning, just to be sure their conversation in the truck the previous day had been real. It was, of course. She knew that. She just…had wanted to see him.

Hannah broke into a wide grin; she couldn't help herself. Albert wanted to court her. He'd offered to join the faith to be with her. It was impossible. She couldn't let herself hope, let herself think what it might be like to cook for Albert, to walk to church with him and to sit with him on snowy winter nights and talk over the day's happenings. But she couldn't help where her mind took her. She imagined him sitting at the head of the table, waiting as she carried a freshly baked sweet potato pie to him. One slice wouldn't do. On second thought, she'd best cut the pie on the counter and bring the plates to the table to keep him from eating the entire thing. The way that man liked to eat, it was a wonder that—

"Han-nah."

She was so surprised by a voice in the garden that she dropped the handful of strawberries she'd just picked. Berries rolled into the plants and spilled between the rows. Hannah let the last two fall and twisted around to see David

King standing a dozen feet away in his Sunday church clothes. "David!" She pressed her strawberry stained fingertips to her beating heart. "You startled me."

David's face froze, mouth open, eyes wide beneath the brim of his straw hat. And just beneath the hat, she could make out a tattered cardboard king's crown. Now that the community knew David liked them, everyone brought them to him whenever they frequented Burger King.

"S…sor-ry." He looked as if he was about to burst into tears.

Hannah rose to her feet, adjusted her apron and brushed the dirt off. "It's all right, David. You didn't do anything wrong. I just didn't know anyone else was in the garden."

"Me. K…King David." He rubbed his hands on his pant legs. Obviously, he had something to say, but she could see that he was nervous.

"What is it, David? Did you come to see Susanna?" Hannah prayed for patience. Had he forgotten that they weren't supposed to see each other until church tomorrow?

*"Ne."* David shook his head. He looked down at his feet and scuffed the toe of one black leather shoe in the dirt. "You. See y…you." Each word was painful. Hannah had to strain to understand him.

"Tell her why!" A new voice, a very familiar

voice, came from behind the big lilac bush on the other side of the garden fence. "Say it!"

David's face turned red. He looked over his shoulder toward the "mysterious" voice coming from the lilac bush, then back at Hannah. "To a... ask you..." He hesitated and chewed at his bottom lip. "Ask you," he repeated.

"Say 'if you can court Susanna!'" Susanna prompted.

David breathed a sigh of relief. "Ifyoucancourt-Susanna," he repeated in a rush. Then, he looked over his shoulder. "I...I told her."

"Shh," Susanna yelled back.

Hannah stared hard at the lilac bush as branches moved on one side, and she caught a glimpse of a navy blue headscarf and a maroon dress. "Susanna?" she called. "Come out here. There's no need for you to hide. I know you're there." It was all she could do not to laugh. This was obviously a joint mission, and there was no doubt who was in charge.

"Not Susanna," came the answer. "Susanna's polishing chairs in the house."

David laughed. "*Ne,* Susanna. You... You're not in the h...house. That's you. I s...see you."

"Susanna," Hannah called. "You may as well come and join us in the garden."

Susanna appeared from behind the bush and reluctantly trudged around the fence to the gate.

"See." David grinned and pointed. His speech was very difficult to comprehend, but Hannah was beginning to be able to understand him. "It is Susanna. She was hiding. Playing a joke on me."

Hannah folded her arms and waited as her daughter came to stand beside David. Susanna's expression was determined, her lips set in a tight line that reminded Hannah of Ruth's mouth when she was displeased. Hannah forced herself to appear serious. "I'm waiting for an explanation," she said to Susanna. Hannah expected Susanna to be contrite, even tearful, as she usually was when caught in mischief, but Hannah was mistaken.

Instead, Susanna boldly reached out and took hold of David's hand. "We're old enough," she declared. "I am not a baby. We want to court like Rebecca. And…" Her blue eyes fixed on David. "Tell her," she urged.

David's mouth opened and closed.

"Tell her we want to get married," Susanna insisted in a loud whisper.

*"Ya,"* he agreed. "To g…get married."

"King David is smart," Susanna said, looking not at Hannah, but at David with shining eyes. "He can read McGuffey fourth reader. By himself."

David shook his head. "Five. I c…can read five."

"And he works hard, don't you?"

"Hard." David grinned and nodded.

Susanna glanced back at her. "And we want… we want to be together. All the time! Him and me. Together."

Hannah's heart sank. They were so young and so determined. And they didn't have the faintest idea how hard marriage was or the challenges they would have to overcome. The idea of allowing Susanna to become a wife was ridiculous…impossible. Yet, Hannah mused, was it any more impossible than what she and Albert were attempting? That Albert become Amish at his age? That the two of them find happiness together? "What does your mother say, David?" Hannah asked.

"She says we should court first," Susanna answered for him. "And we want…" She stared hard at David. When he didn't speak, she tilted her head and looked directly into his face. "The frolic," she hinted. "Wednesday."

It took Hannah only seconds to realize that Susanna was talking about the young people's singing and haystack supper that Lydia and her husband were hosting Friday evening. Any date in the future was always Wednesday in Susanna's mind.

"Tell her!" Susanna insisted.

"We w…want to go," David said in a loud voice. "Her and me. T…together."

Hannah looked from one eager face to the other. And felt herself soften. Maybe she had been wrong. Was Albert right? In her desire to protect Susanna, was she preventing her from living a full life? Didn't Susanna deserve the same chance at happiness that she wanted for all her daughters? That she wanted for herself? "All right," she agreed. "You and David may go to the Beachys' singing, but you will go with Charley and Miriam, and you will behave yourself. Do you understand?"

*"Ya, Mam,"* Susanna said.

"We w...will." David nodded.

"And there will be no kissing. Not when people are looking, and not when they aren't."

*"Ne,"* Susanna promised. She raised a warning finger and shook it in David's face. "No kissing. You understand?"

He nodded even more vigorously.

Hannah put her hands on her hips. "Friday night." She glanced at Susanna. "As for you, so long as you're here, I presume you've finished polishing the furniture. You may help me pick the rest of these strawberries."

Susanna sighed. "Go home, King David," she ordered. "But come talk to me tomorrow at church. It's church Sunday. And come back Friday."

Obediently, David strode away.

"Bye," Susanna called after him. "Bye."

David waved back. He was grinning from ear to ear.

"Strawberries," Hannah reminded her daughter.

Susanna knelt and began to pick the fat berries, but she was humming an off-key tune under her breath, and Hannah could just make out the repeated words. "First courting, then married, first courting, then…"

Hannah rolled her eyes and gazed skyward. *What have I just agreed to? Pray God I won't live to regret it.*

# Chapter Thirteen

On Friday evening, nearly a week later, Albert and Hannah rode with John in his truck to Samuel's home. The days since he and Hannah had run through the rain together had passed quickly. Each evening and three of the mornings, he'd come to the farm to care for the alpacas, and he and Hannah had talked, not of serious matters but of everyday occurrences—the difficult delivery of twin calves, his great nephew 'Kota's progress at school, a much-looked-for letter Hannah had received from her daughter in Brazil.

He and Hannah had not held hands again or touched, but Albert had savored the intimacy of having someone who listened to him and cared about him. Hannah had invited him for breakfasts and suppers, always surrounded by family and friends, always careful not to do anything that would compromise the fragile relationship that was rapidly growing between them.

They'd not discussed the proposal he was about to make to her church, but it remained central in his thoughts, as he suspected it did in Hannah's. And even with his hopes and future in turmoil, Albert had closed his eyes each night at peace with himself and utterly happy. He'd always found fulfillment in his work and in the love he felt from John, Grace and little 'Kota, but this feeling for Hannah was something he'd never known before and it was precious.

On Sunday last, Albert had attended the morning Mennonite worship service with John and his family as he did every Sunday, but he'd refrained from speaking to his pastor or neighbors about his desire to court Hannah Yoder. He hadn't done so to hide his intentions, but because, at least for the present, it was a private matter between him, Hannah and God. Afterward, Ted, one of Albert's acquaintances from church, invited him to join them for dinner. Ted's sister, an attractive, forty-year-old RN who Albert had met several years ago, would be there. Ted hinted that she and Albert might be compatible. Albert gently refused the invitation. Courtship with a suitable Mennonite woman would be simpler, but she wouldn't be Hannah, and the more he thought about it, the surer he was that his future lay with her and the Amish.

When Hannah had insisted midweek that she wanted to come with him and John to speak to Samuel, Albert hadn't been able to hide his surprise. *Of course,* he'd replied, *whatever you want. I didn't think that you...* He'd felt his throat and face grow warm. *That you'd...*

His Hannah had laughed. *Albert. I'm not a shy, young* maedle. *And if there's a case to be made for you, I need to be there with you to speak to our deacon.*

Funny how Samuel Mast, Hannah's son-in-law, neighbor and longtime friend, had become someone to be approached with trepidation. Among the Seven Poplar Amish, the position of deacon was one of great authority. He was the enforcer of rules and the first member of the elders to contact a church member about possible wayward behavior. Bishop Atlee would make the final decision as to whether or not Albert and Hannah would be able to court, and his judgment would be final. But before that, the bishop would likely talk over the matter with Samuel and the two preachers, Caleb Wittner and Reuben Coblentz.

Albert and John had waited until 7:00 p.m. to pick up Hannah so that Samuel and Anna would be finished with the evening meal and chores. Wondering if Hannah was as nervous as he was, Albert glanced at her as John pulled into the Mast lane. None of them had spoken in the short ride around the corner from Hannah's to Samuel's place. Hannah sat on the truck seat between them, tall and serene, her hands folded in her lap. She wore a blue dress, a black apron and a black bonnet over her starched white *kapp.* Albert was glad that he'd taken the trouble to change into his Sunday clothes, a black suit, a tie and a white shirt.

John parked the truck in the yard, and the three got out. "You look nice," Albert whispered to Hannah, and was rewarded by a warm smile.

"You, too," she teased. "You *redd* up nicely."

They stood together in the driveway. "You're with me on this?" he asked.

A pink flush tinted her cheeks. "*Ya,* Albert," she answered softly. "On this, we are together." Her expression grew serious. "But remember, I am agreeing only to walk out with you, to see if our feelings are real, if this is the right thing for us. And only if there's hope for a future for us here in Seven Poplars."

"I understand. I already think it is the right thing for us—I'm sure it is. But being together—courting—will make certain that we aren't being hasty."

"One step at a time," she insisted. She was standing close to him, and for an instant, Albert thought that she might take his arm, but she didn't. "If the Lord wills it," she whispered. "Last night, I prayed for guidance."

"Me, too." He smiled at her. "On my knees, and that isn't as easy as it once was."

She chuckled. "I've seen you lift fifty-pound bags of alpaca feed, and I've watched you pitch in to help with the haying. Any man who can throw bales of hay all afternoon onto a wagon isn't ready for a rocking chair."

"Are you two coming?" John called from the porch. "Or are you going to make me do this by myself?"

"We're coming." Albert's hands felt damp and he rubbed them nervously against his trouser legs. He could feel his pulse racing. Hannah had put it right, as always. This was the first step. They would take the journey together, one step at a time. And if things worked out, he would know that he was doing the right thing for both of them…and following the path that God had mapped out for him from the start.

"John!" Hannah's daughter Anna opened the door. "Come in!" She caught sight of Albert and her mother. "Albert! *Mam!* What a nice surprise!" She ushered them in with a wide smile and a genuine hug for her mother.

Usually the Amish that Albert knew were shy about showing affection in public, but Hannah's family was different. She, her daughters and her grandchildren were open about their love for each other. He liked that, and, next to John's Grace—

Anna was his favorite among Hannah's children. Anna had a way of making everyone feel so welcome.

"Samuel!" Anna called. "We have company." She noticed Albert's suit and exchanged a glance with her mother. "And I think maybe they've come to talk with you."

Propane lamps cast light around the huge, spotless kitchen. Samuel, shoes off, had been sitting in his chair with a toddler on his lap. There were children of various ages sprawled on the floor playing Dutch Blitz; a girl was curled up in a window seat with a book. Albert didn't see Hannah's mother-in-law, who lived here with them.

As if reading his thoughts, Hannah asked, "Where's Lovina? She's not under the weather, is she?"

Anna chuckled and shook her head. "*Ne, Grossmama* is *gut.* Tonight is an open house at the Englisher senior center where she teaches her rug making. They wanted her to give a demonstration. The center's van came for her and will bring her home."

Albert remembered that Hannah had told him that it was Anna who'd gone over Samuel's head to the bishop to ask permission for her grandmother to attend the senior center. Clearly, it had been a good thing for the aging woman because Hannah insisted that Lovina's memory seemed stable, and her periods of dementia troubled her less often since she'd started going there. Albert took heart from that. Maybe seeing how the elderly Lovina had benefited from bending the community rules and allowing her to associate with the English community would make Samuel more inclined to support his courtship of Hannah. If Samuel was in favor, it would help their cause.

"Actually, we did come to speak with Samuel," John said after the usual greetings were exchanged, as well as inquiries about everyone's health and a discussion of the weather and other general topics. Albert was well aware that no business could be conducted with the Amish until courtesies were observed.

"Of course," Anna said. "Children!" She motioned to them. "Your father has—"

"No need for them to put away their games," Samuel said. "There's yet an hour or so before bedtime. We'll go into the parlor."

"I'll bring coffee," Anna offered. "And rhubarb pie." John started to decline, but Anna wouldn't allow it. "Nonsense," she said. "I've never known you or your uncle to turn down a slice of pie."

Samuel led the way to the formal parlor, a room at the front of the house with double doors that opened to provide a large space for religious services.

"Uncle Albert wants to make a request," John said. "And he'd like you to take it to the church elders."

"Sit, please, everyone." Samuel sat in a recliner and placed the reading glasses in his hand on a table beside an old German Bible. "Now tell me, Albert," he said when the three of them had sat on the couch across from him. "What important matter has brought you three to my door tonight?"

Hesitantly, at first, and then with more confidence, Albert began to explain how he and Hannah wanted permission to court and how he wanted to be considered for membership in the Amish church. "I realize that my veterinary practice could be an issue," he said. "It's something that I've given a lot of thought to, and I would be willing to do whatever is necessary to become a part of the community."

Samuel's brow furrowed, and he stroked his whiskered chin thoughtfully. "You want to court Hannah?" he repeated. "And you want to become Amish?"

"I do," Albert answered. "My family roots lie with the faith."

There was a knock at the parlor door and Anna called softly, "Samuel? I've brought the coffee and pie."

Samuel got up and went to take the heavy tray from her. "Best make another pot, wife," he said, glancing in his guests' direction. "I think we're going to be here awhile."

The following morning, Hannah, Sara, Susanna and Ellie left early to go to Ruth and Miriam's house to put up some early string beans. Together they snapped the beans, packed them into canning jars and processed them in a pressure cooker. It was time-consuming work but satisfying, because the results were lovely quarts of vegetables that would keep all winter. Hannah was glad for the opportunity to be with her daughters and friends and happier still to be busy.

Miriam's husband Charley came into the house midmorning and said that Irwin had made a minor repair to the alpacas' fence as instructed. He'd also mentioned that Albert had come by earlier to feed and care for the animals.

Hannah was sorry that she hadn't been home and had the chance to speak to Albert that morning. Even if they couldn't spend private time together while Samuel was considering their case, she looked forward to seeing Albert when he came to tend to the alpacas. Sometimes just catching a glimpse of him pulling into the yard made her smile.

Samuel hadn't given them an answer the previous night, but Hannah really hadn't expected one. He took his position of deacon seriously and wasn't a man to make snap decisions. She'd explained to Albert that Samuel would want to consider their proposal seriously and pray on it before responding. And she'd warned Albert that a final answer from the bishop might take weeks or even months. Old Order Amish didn't stray from the accustomed way of doing things easily or often. And if she were to make a guess, she would think that the bishop would refuse to allow the two of them to walk out together. But Albert had seemed so hopeful that she didn't want to say so. Still, she couldn't help being just a little sorry that she didn't have a cell phone. It would have been nice to hear Albert's voice, even if they couldn't see each other in person.

The following day was a visiting Sunday rather than a day of worship, and Johanna and Roland had invited the whole family, including Sara and Ellie, and Aunt Jezzy and her husband, to their house for a potluck picnic lunch. Roland, Charley and Eli set up tables outside, and Johanna had prepared ham and chicken salad sandwiches and gallons of lemonade and iced tea. Rebecca had baked three sheet cakes, and Miriam and Ruth had brought potato salad, coleslaw and green bean salad. Grace, John and 'Kota had been invited, and 'Kota was eager to play with all his cousins, especially Johanna's boys, J.J. and Jonah, who were close in age. Roland had built a child-size sulky cart with a wide bench seat so that the kids could take turns pulling each other around the farm.

Soon babies were playing on blankets, toddlers trailing after older children and the men were sitting under the trees with glasses of cool drinks. Hannah's girls, all but Anna, were busy going in and out of the house carrying food. "I wonder where Anna can be," Johanna said to Grace. "I told her that we'd be eating early. We'll have no peace until the children and husbands are fed." She smiled at her mother. "Honestly, I don't know how you managed all those years. Sometimes, I think Roland is worse than the kids about eating. He's hungry all the time."

"He works hard," Hannah said.

"He does," Johanna agreed. "He's a good man, *Mam.* Maybe better than I deserve."

"Never say that." Hannah hugged her. "You've had your share of troubles. It's so good to see you happy. And you are, aren't you? Truly happy in your marriage?"

Johanna nodded and hugged her back. "Truly, *Mam.* I'm just sorry it took so long for me to realize what a treasure he is."

"For everything there is a time," Hannah said. "You've wept bitter tears, now this is your time to find laughter." She glanced at Rebecca who was whispering to Miriam and giggling. Hannah didn't need to ask Rebecca if she was pleased with her new bridegroom. The joy in her eyes said it all.

"Anna and Samuel are finally here!" Grace called. "They've brought two buggies, so *Grossmama* must be with them."

Hannah hurried outside after her daughter to meet Anna, Lovina and all the grandchildren. Anna handed Rose to her and then helped *Grossmama* to climb down out of the buggy. Behind them, Rudy reined the other horse and buggy to a walk. As the vehicle rolled past, Hannah gasped in surprise. Albert was seated on the front seat beside a grinning Rudy.

"Samuel invited him," Anna murmured to Hannah.

"Samuel did?" *Did this mean that Samuel approved of them?* She bounced Rose against her shoulder, nuzzling her neck, glad to have the little girl to hide behind.

"It's a picnic, *Mam,*" Anna said. Her large, blue eyes twinkled with mischief. "Grace and John and 'Kota are here. Why not Albert?"

*"Ya."* Hannah nodded. "Why not Albert?"

Peter opened the door at the back of the buggy and lifted out a tall stack of pizza boxes. "Albert brought pizza," he announced.

Johanna's Jonah shrieked with excitement. "Pizza!" he cried. "J.J.! 'Kota! We're having pizza!"

Albert approached Hannah. "I hope it's all right that I came."

"And why wouldn't it be? How many times have you shared our meals?" Anna asked as she assisted her grandmother to a comfortable chair. Almost before Lovina was seated, one of Anna's girls came with a tall glass of lemonade for her.

"Pizza pie," Lovina grumbled. "Store-bought Englisher food. My father would never have permitted his children to eat it. But nobody stays by the old ways anymore. And nobody listens to me." She scowled. "This lemonade needs more sugar, Hannah. Did Hannah make it? She makes lemonade so sour it puckers your mouth like green persimmons."

"I'll sweeten it for you, *schweschter*." Aunt Jezzy reached for the glass.

"*Ne,* no need to make a fuss over me. I'll drink it like it is," the old lady conceded with a sigh.

Hannah looked up at Albert. "There are some chairs in the kitchen that need to come outside. Would you mind helping me?"

"Anything I can do to help."

She went into the house followed closely by Albert. "It was good of you to think of pizza," she said. "The children will love it."

"Your mother-in-law doesn't seem too happy that I brought it," he said.

Hannah glanced back over her shoulder at him and chuckled. "Lovina loves pizza. Wait until you see how many pieces she eats." When they got inside, the kitchen was deserted. "Do you think it's a good sign that Samuel invited you?" she asked in a low voice as she turned to him. "I'm so glad you accepted. I'm sorry we missed each other yesterday."

"Me, too," he said. "Samuel called me on my cell phone. I suppose he must have used the phone at the chair shop. He said that I was a good friend and part of the family, no matter what the bishop decided."

"He couldn't have spoken to Bishop Atlee yet."

Albert shrugged. "I think he did. One of the twins said their father went out early this morning. He didn't say where he was going, but he put on his black coat and good hat before he left."

An emptiness settled in the pit of Hannah's stomach. "*Ach,* I didn't think he would say anything so soon. He'd want to talk with Reuben and Caleb, too." Goose bumps rose on her arms and she rubbed at them.

"Don't worry. Your bishop is a reasonable man. We've always gotten along well."

"*Ya,* I suppose." Hannah's gaze met his and they stood there for what seemed like hours, although it could only have been seconds. Hannah's heart was beating fast, and she could feel the heat on her face and throat.

*Was* it possible? Would Bishop Atlee approve? Would this wonderful man give up everything he'd ever known to be her husband and join her church?

"This will all work out. I'm sure of it." Albert took her hand. "Because I…I love you, Hannah. And I want you to be my wife."

"Do you understand what that would mean?" she murmured. His grip tightened on her fingers and she went on. "If you marry me, Albert, you marry my whole family, my children and my grandchildren. Do you think you can love them, too?"

"I'd consider it an honor," he answered. "I'd never try to take Jonas's place, but maybe they could find a place in their hearts for me, as well."

Hannah felt light enough to float off the floor. She opened her mouth to tell him that she loved him, too, but before she could, the moment was broken as Susanna charged into the kitchen. Hannah snatched her hand from Albert's, hoping the daughter she'd been admonishing for improper behavior hadn't caught her.

"*Mam! Mam!* King David is here. He came." Susanna's face glowed and she clapped her hands. "He said he would sit with me. To eat."

"I told you they were coming. Lydia told me that you two were very well behaved at the singing. That shows me that you listened. So, I thought you might enjoy having David eat with us today."

*"Ya!"* Susanna hopped from one foot to the other with excitement. "I was *gut*. I remembered what you said. Courting. Not kissing. *No* kissing." She shook her index finger for emphasis. "And no hand holding." She spun around and raced out the door.

Albert chuckled, watching Susanna go. "That sounds like good advice." He glanced at Hannah and winked. "For more people than Susanna and David."

Hannah tried not to let her amusement show as she raised a finger to her lips. "Shh." Albert grinned, and Hannah couldn't help thinking what a good-looking man he was. Not flashy handsome, but solid and dependable-looking with a strong chin and kind eyes.

It was worldly to judge people by their outward appearance, but Hannah had always liked men with strong chins. It was difficult to take a man seriously if he had weak features. It was obvious that Albert had shaved this morning, but he already had the faint shadow of a beard. She was sure that Albert could grow a good, thick beard, and he would need to if they married. All Amish married men had beards, even if some were a little thin and straggly.

"Let's eat," Johanna called through the door. "*Mam!* Are you getting the chairs?"

"I think we'd better get outside," Albert said as he picked up the chairs Hannah pointed to. "Before we cause a scandal."

Hannah smiled. "I'm afraid it's too late for that, Albert."

# Chapter Fourteen

The afternoon picnic was everything Hannah could have wished for. Dinner went off smoothly. Babies slept, children laughed and played, dogs barked and chased rabbits, led by Albert's hound, old Blue, who had come in the carriage with him. The women talked and soothed kids' scraped knees and hurt feelings. After the last dessert had been admired and eaten, the men offered to clear away and wash the dishes, a task the wives, daughters and neighbor women were happy to delegate. After the chores were done, Charley and Eli challenged all comers to a horseshoe throwing match, and all the men, including Albert, enthusiastically headed to the horseshoe pits, leaving Sara, Aunt Jezzy, Sadie, Hannah and her daughters and their new friend Ellie to sit under the trees with their shoes off and sip iced tea. Even Lovina had stopped grumbling and drifted off into a deep sleep, causing not a few smiles by her loud snoring.

"*Mam*," Johanna said. "I think we need more lemonade. Do you mind coming in and helping make some?"

Hannah looked at her quizzically. She was sure that she'd seen another two gallons of lemonade standing ready on the kitchen counter.

"I'll help," Miriam offered, rising quickly to her feet. She cut her eyes meaningfully toward the kitchen door, and Hannah realized that the girls were trying to get her alone. Nodding, Hannah rose and went inside.

Rebecca and Anna were already waiting for them. "What did Samuel say?" Rebecca demanded eagerly. "Anna said he went to the bishop this morning."

Hannah looked from one daughter to the other as Ruth entered the room.

"Come clean, *Mam*," Miriam said. "We've all been wondering what's been going on between you and Albert. We couldn't imagine what you were thinking. But then Anna said that Albert has offered to become Amish. That's wonderful. I can't believe it." She clasped her hands. "He's perfect for us."

Suddenly weak-kneed, Hannah dropped to a high kitchen stool and looked at Anna. "You told them?"

A smile spread over Anna's round face. "Better I tell them what's really happening than they think the worst—that you were going to abandon us and turn Mennonite."

"And would that be the worst?" Hannah said. "If I went back to being Mennonite?" She looked from one daughter to the next.

"You've been baptized, *Mam.* You know what that would mean," Rebecca said gently. "It's not the same thing as Grace or Leah becoming Mennonite."

They were right, of course. "Be at ease, daughters. I've given my promise, to all of you and to God. Amish I am, and Amish I will remain."

"So Albert's courting you?" Miriam said. "Were you trying to keep that a secret from us?"

Ruth snickered. "Look who's talking about keeping secrets, sister."

"I was going to tell her today," Miriam said.

Hannah stared at her. "Tell me what?"

Miriam could hardly contain her giggles. "I'm sorry, *Mam.* It's just that after the last time that we thought I was, it turned out to be a false alarm."

"Will you just tell her and get it over with," Rebecca urged excitedly.

Miriam let out a dramatic sigh. "Charley didn't want to disappoint anyone again, so that's why we waited. But this time it's for sure." She threw up her hands. "We're going to be parents."

"You're having a baby!" Hannah got up and enveloped Miriam in a bear hug. "That's wonderful!"

Miriam laughed and hugged her mother. "It is, isn't it? I've seen the midwife three times and she heard a strong heartbeat. Just one baby, though." She cut her eyes at her sister. "I was afraid I'd have twins like Ruth." She laughed again. "Charley was hoping for twins, but one at a time is plenty for me."

Hannah looked suspiciously at her daughters. "And who else knows?"

"Just us," Anna replied. She'd found a dishcloth and was wiping down the counter. "And Charley and Eli. And Samuel. And Grace, of course. Not Leah, because it takes so long for letters to get back and forth. And we didn't tell Susanna because you know she can't keep a secret for two minutes. The whole church would know. Oh, and our Naomi. There isn't much that goes on that she misses."

"The whole community will know soon enough." Miriam patted her midsection, which Hannah realized *did* look thicker than usual. "We're ready, *Mam.* Charley and I are."

"I'm so happy for you," Hannah said.

"So let's get back to Albert." Miriam glanced toward the door. "It makes me happy to hear that you're ready. To think of marrying again."

Hannah sat down on the stool again and folded her arms, not wanting her girls to see how vulnerable she felt right now about her and Albert, or how much she wanted their approval. "I think I am ready to have someone again, to be with Albert." She glanced into their faces, afraid of what she might see there. "Do you mind terribly? It's not that I've forgotten your father. I could never do that."

"We know," Ruth assured her, looking around at her sisters. "We all agree it's been a long time. We've been holding our breath, afraid that you'd choose someone we didn't like or some man from another state and you'd have to leave us. But Albert, he'll make a good stepfather—provided he joins the church."

"So long as the bishop permits it," Miriam added. "Samuel didn't say he wouldn't, did he?"

"Samuel was shocked at first," Anna admitted. "You know how Samuel can be, but he thinks it should be considered, otherwise he wouldn't have gone to Bishop Atlee. Of course you know Uncle Reuben will be against it. Aunt Martha leads him around by the nose." She grimaced. "She makes *Grossmama* seem like a spring lamb for contrariness, at least where any of us are concerned."

"But Caleb will have a say." Ruth paused, broom in hand, and glanced at Rebecca. "What do you suppose he'll think of all this?"

Rebecca shook her head. "I don't know. He hasn't been a preacher that long. I imagine he'll pray on it, give his counsel and then go along with whatever Bishop Atlee decides to do."

"Could he do it?" Miriam asked between sips of water. "Albert? Could he give up his Englisher life? His truck? Electricity? And what about his job?" She shook her head. "It won't be easy." She hesitated. "Will Albert want to take over the farm?"

"We haven't talked about any of that. Not yet. We only agreed we'd like to court to see if marriage would suit us. But if Albert does want to farm, he has his own land. Don't worry. Our farm will always be your home."

Miriam nodded. "That's good to know, because Charley has his heart in that land." She smiled. "And so do I." She went to the refrigerator. "Are there any sweet pickles left, Johanna? Oh, there they are, stuck behind the relish."

"She's eating pickles all the time," Ruth put in. "It's going to be a boy."

"It would mean so much to me if I know that you girls support me in this," Hannah said. "That you approve of Albert."

"Of course, we do, *Mam,*" Anna assured her. "He's a good man, even if he is a Mennonite." She laughed again, and her sisters chuckled with her. "You know I don't mean that in a bad way.

We can see that he makes you happy, and that's what's important to us."

"Besides," Miriam added. "He'll be handy to have around when our livestock has an injury."

"Well, we shall see." Hannah rose from the stool. "We'd better get back to the others. See if the twins are up from their nap. Maybe check out that horseshoe game?" As she started for the door, she heard a baby wail. "Told you," she said.

When all the babies had been changed and fed, the younger boys told to take their ball game farther from the house and the little girls entranced by a story that Ellie was telling them, Hannah, Rebecca, Sara and Lovina walked toward the area where the men were pitching horseshoes. They were halfway across the barnyard when a horse and carriage came up the lane.

"I wonder who that can be." Hannah turned to get a better look. "I don't recognize the sorrel."

"It's Bishop Atlee's buggy," Rebecca said. "Caleb mentioned he just bought a new sorrel pacer."

"The bishop?" Lovina's hand flew to her *kapp*. She patted it to make certain it was on straight and then tied her strings tightly under her chin. "He's come to help Jonas milk the cows," she said. "Such a nice young man, Bishop Mordecai. He wanted to court me, you know. But I'd set my *kapp* for Jonas's father."

"That's our bishop, Bishop Atlee, *Grossmama*,"

Rebecca reminded her gently. "Bishop Mordecai passed away when *Dat* was a baby."

Hannah watched as the bishop came toward them in the driveway. Tentatively, she raised her hand to wave. He nodded, reined the sorrel to a walk, and drove past them. Had his expression been stern?

"I'm sure you're wrong," Lovina said. "I think I know Bishop Mordecai when I see him."

Hannah quickened her step. As she approached the gathering of men at the horseshoe pits, she saw that Albert was showing David how to improve his pitch. David flung the first shoe far to the left of the peg. But his second horseshoe flew gracefully in an arc and dropped around the peg. It spun several times and came to rest firmly on the peg. David let out a yelp of pure joy and began to jump up and down.

Susanna ran out to the peg, grabbed the horseshoe and waved it in the air. "He scored!" she yelled. "My David made a home run!"

David beamed with pride as his father, Albert and Hannah's sons-in-law praised him and patted him on the back. "Did you see?" David shouted to Susanna. "Did you see me, Susanna?"

"*Ya!* I did see!" Susanna replied. She glanced around, realized that she was standing in the center of the horseshoe pits and hurried toward

Hannah, still holding the horseshoe. "David won," she declared. "My David won."

Hannah nodded, but her gaze followed Albert as he walked away from the others toward Bishop Atlee, who had gotten out of his buggy. Apparently, the bishop had known Albert would be there today and had come to talk to him. Hannah's heart sank. No positive decision could have been made so quickly. He must have come to forbid Albert from seeing her. She felt sick.

"It doesn't have to be bad news," Sara said softly in Hannah's ear.

"I know," Hannah replied, "but tell my stomach that." She wished she hadn't eaten so much at lunch. Her chest felt as though it was full of butterflies.

The waiting was awful. Sara kept trying to keep her from thinking the worst, but Hannah felt as though everyone was looking at her. Why hadn't Bishop Atlee asked to speak with them both? It wasn't as if this decision didn't affect her as much as it did Albert. She wanted to explain her position to the bishop, but it would be impolite to intrude on his conversation with Albert, and she didn't want either of them to think badly of her.

"This sun is really warm today, isn't it?" Sara remarked. "Wisconsin summers can be brutal, but it doesn't get this hot in June. Let's go back and sit under the trees."

Hannah glanced at Albert and the bishop speaking privately. "Am I being a fool, Sara?" she asked.

"*Ne,* my friend," Sara answered, patting Hannah's arm. "We have to keep hoping for the best. As I do with Ellie."

Hannah realized that she hadn't asked Sara how the interview went with Ellie's prospective husband. Sara was careful not to divulge personal information about her clients, and Hannah didn't want to pry, but she felt as though she'd been so wrapped up in her own life that she hadn't considered Sara's. Ellie hadn't said anything, but she had seemed happy today. "Your match, for Ellie," Hannah said. "Is it going well?"

Sara grimaced. "Actually, it isn't going at all. The family was pleased with her and the boy seemed willing, but Ellie refused him. She said she didn't think they were *compatible.*" Sara arched her dark eyebrows. "Ellie's father and mother will be disappointed, but eventually I'll find her a husband. I always do." She lifted her chin. "Look, I think your Albert is coming this way."

Hannah looked up, and saw Albert and his dog walking in her direction. Sara discreetly moved away to speak to Lovina. Bishop Atlee joined the men, and someone handed him a glass of iced tea. Hannah could hear the bishop's voice, but couldn't make out what he was saying.

Albert stopped in front of her. Old Blue, who'd been trailing behind him, dropped at his feet. "Do you feel all right, Hannah? You look as though you've seen a ghost."

"What did he say?" She tried desperately to maintain her composure.

"About what I expected. He wants to pray on it. And to talk to Samuel and his preachers some more. But he didn't say no. He listened to me, and he advised us to both think carefully about our decision." Albert breathed a sigh of relief. "In the meantime, he said that I was free to *walk out* with you until the council of elders reaches a conclusion." His smile became a grin. "So long as we maintain decent and proper behavior."

Hannah smiled, suddenly feeling shy. "And can we?"

Albert chuckled. "We can try, Hannah. We can try."

And try they did. Albert continued to come mornings and evenings to care for the alpacas, and Hannah was careful to be sure they remained outside in the yard when he was on the farm unless two other people were present. If Irwin and Susanna were there for breakfast and, or supper, she would invite Albert, and he would accept.

Sara and Ellie returned to Wisconsin the Tuesday following the family picnic. Sara hadn't signed a contract on property in Kent County, but she'd told Hannah that she would be moving to Delaware soon. Final arrangements would depend on negotiations with her late husband's sons and whether or not she had to sell the farm where she presently lived. Hannah was sorry to see both of them go. She'd grown quite fond of Ellie and had hoped that she would become a part of the Seven Poplars community, too. As for Sara, the sooner she returned, the better. As much as she valued her good friends, Lydia Beachy and Fannie Byler, Sara was special. When she left, Hannah assured her that she was welcome to come back and stay as long as she liked.

Wednesday was a workday at the schoolhouse. With school out for the summer, there was painting and general maintenance to do, and Charley had recruited the Gleaners, the local Amish youth group, to help. Hannah and the girls scrubbed windows, polished woodwork, desks and cleaned out the cast-iron wood stove. Hannah hadn't expected Albert to come, as she'd supposed that he would be busy with his veterinary practice, but he arrived, toolbox in hand, ready to do whatever he could to help. It turned out that Albert was handier than Hannah had suspected. He fixed the drawer that was sticking in her teacher's desk, and made some much-needed repairs to chair-and-desk combinations. Finally, he and Irwin had surprised her by installing, along the back wall of the schoolhouse, a six-by-ten-foot old-fashioned blackboard that he'd found free on the Internet.

"You never cease to amaze me," Hannah declared when the project was complete.

"You thought doctoring animals was my only skill?" Albert grinned, clearly pleased by her praise. "I wasn't always a vet," he reminded her. "And remember, I grew up on a farm. I can still swing a hammer."

Ten minutes later, a pizza delivery boy drove into the school driveway with a stack of hot pizzas. The treat was much appreciated by Charley and the Gleaners, who washed their lunch down with cold well water. "You'll spoil them," Hannah warned Albert. "They'll start expecting pizza every time you attend an event."

Albert grinned and shrugged. "Better that than if I'd baked them cupcakes. My father and I used to argue over which of us was the worst cook. The truth is, I'm pretty sad."

"Is that why you want to marry me?" she teased as she reached for another slice of mushroom-and-sausage pizza. "For my cooking?"

He smiled. "Marriages have been made for worse things."

On Saturday, Albert rented a fifteen-passenger van and took Hannah, Grace, Susanna and David, Johanna and her three children, 'Kota, Anna's twins, and Rebecca and Amelia to the Salisbury Zoo. It was next to a small park with lots of trees, a large playground and a picnic area where they could eat the big lunch that the women had packed. The zoo was a small one, featuring South American animals, and the children were fascinated by the monkeys, alligators and lizards, which were like those their Aunt Leah described in her letters.

But as much as the children enjoyed the exotic animals, the otters were hands down their favorites. Hannah couldn't even find it in her heart to admonish Susanna when she and David stood side by side, holding hands, fascinated by the antics of the playful mammals. Parts of the otter habitat had been fashioned to replicate a fast-running stream, complete with water slide, and the excited giggles and squeals of her grandchildren delighted Hannah.

"Are you having a good time?" Hannah asked Albert. "I am. It was so thoughtful of you to arrange this trip for us."

'Kota tugged at his hand. "Uncle Albert, look! The sign says there are llamas. Can we go see the llamas? They're like alpacas, but different. Mom says they're bigger."

"We'll see everything. I promise you," Grace assured her son. "You'll wear Uncle Albert out. A few more minutes, and then we'll go on to the bison."

"J.J. and I want to see the llamas," 'Kota pestered.

"You'll wait for the rest of us," Grace warned him quietly. "Why don't you two go on," she urged Hannah and Albert. "We can manage the children. Take some time for yourselves. We're in a public park. It's perfectly permissible."

Hannah glanced at Susanna and David.

"And I'll look after those two," Rebecca promised. "Go while you have the chance. We'll catch up with you in the picnic area."

Hannah looked at Albert for confirmation. "We'll take you up on that offer. I'm sure Albert's ready for a few moments of peace."

"Whatever you want," Albert said. "I'm good."

Hannah nodded. "But you'd be better with a little quiet." He didn't protest when she walked away.

They walked for a while, side by side, until they came to a bench, surrounded by flowering trees and bushes. They sat there in comfortable silence for nearly half an hour, not talking, just looking at the birds in the trees, and watching the other visitors wander past. It was a good feeling. Hannah liked this about Albert. He didn't always have to be talking. There was something intimate about being near one another, experiencing new sights and sounds, learning more about each other.

"I'll make you happy, Hannah," he said finally, turning to look at her. "At least, I'll do my best."

She met his gaze. "And you don't mind giving up your life for us to be together?"

"When I'm with you, Hannah, I don't feel as though I'd be giving up anything. Having peace, family, not being alone—it's what I've always wanted."

"And the Amish faith? Do you think you could accept it? Accept the *Ordnung?* Obey the wishes of the elders and the community?"

"I think it feels right," he admitted. "No matter what, I think it's what I need to do. And being part of your family, it's almost too much to ask."

She sighed. "You realize the bishop could refuse us. And then, I'd have no choice. I'd go on loving you, Albert, but it would mean we couldn't be together."

"I understand." He nodded. "It's a chance I have to take."

She cradled her hands in her lap and looked up into his face. "I'm afraid," she admitted. "I want to have faith, but I'm afraid we're asking too much." She swallowed the lump rising in her throat. "You know that even if the elders agree, we would have to wait at least a year."

"It would be hard, because I want to marry you now," he said. "I'd marry you today if I could. But it will be worth every moment, because I know that at the end of the time, we'll be husband and wife."

"Then we'll keep praying," she agreed, trying to find the confidence he seemed to feel. "And hope that whatever happens, we'll have the faith to accept the answer and live with it."

"We'll keep praying," he agreed. "And in the—"

"Hannah! Come quick!" Anna's Rudy came running toward them. His face was as red as his hair, and he'd lost his straw hat. "It's Susanna!" he shouted. "She fell down the steps! Johanna thinks her arm is broken!"

# Chapter Fifteen

Albert heard Susanna shrieking before they reached her. Grace and Johanna had her seated on the ground, her injured arm in her lap. They were attempting to soothe her, but Susanna was either suffering intense pain or she was hysterical. The younger children sat solemnly on the steps with Rebecca, staring at Susanna.

"Thank goodness you're here." Grace stood up. "I'm pretty sure that her arm is broken."

Hannah crouched beside her youngest daughter. "Hush now, Susanna. It will be all right. No need to carry on so. You'll upset all the animals. You don't want to do that, do you?" She rested a hand on the back of Susanna's shoulder. "Show me where it hurts."

"My...my arm!" Susanna wailed.

Hannah's eyes showed her concern, but she remained calm and kept her voice low. "Tell me what happened, Susanna." She took her chin and lifted it so that she could command all of her attention.

"I fell." Susanna was sobbing now, her face red, great tears streaming down her cheeks. "It hurts!"

Hannah glanced around. "Where's David?"

"He got upset and felt sick to his stomach," Johanna said. "Peter took him to the restroom."

"Could you look at her arm, Albert?" Hannah asked. "I don't see anything definite other than bruising, but you would know better."

"He's an animal doctor, not a people doctor," 'Kota remarked loudly.

Grace raised a finger in warning. "Hush, now. Uncle Albert knows about bones."

Albert moved toward Susanna to inspect her arm. "And bones are bones." He lowered himself to his knees, looking directly into her eyes. "Now, I'm going to touch your arm," he quietly told her. "But I promise, I'll be very gentle."

Susanna shook her head and shrank back against her mother. "*Ne! Ne!* I want David. My David," she sobbed.

Albert exchanged glances with Hannah. "All right, Susanna," he said. "I won't touch it if you don't want me to." He didn't really need to. The slight misalignment of her forearm spoke for itself. Fortunately, there was no break in the skin, so it was a simple fracture rather than a compound one. "She needs to go to an E.R. or an urgent-care facility."

"Should we call an ambulance?" Grace asked. "I have my cell phone."

"I don't think that's necessary." Albert stood up. He knew that Hannah, like the majority of the Old Order Amish, carried no health insurance. Even a short ambulance ride would cost her hundreds of dollars. "There's an excellent hospital within a half a mile of here. We can drive her there." He looked at Johanna. "It might be better if the rest of you remained here."

"Absolutely," Hannah agreed. "No need to overwhelm the hospital staff. Besides, these children are hungry. They need their lunch, and they may as well enjoy the playground, as we promised. If Susanna's arm is broken, it will take time to have it x-rayed and cast. The family may as well spend the rest of the afternoon here at the zoo."

"If you're sure you don't need me, *Mam,*" Johanna said. "I agree that the hospital waiting room isn't the best place for all of us. We can all say a prayer for Susanna before lunch."

"It's settled, then." Albert put his hands together. "Susanna, do you think you can walk?"

"It hurts!" Susanna cried and again began to sob.

"Susanna, listen to me." Hannah planted a kiss on the top of her head. "Big girls grit their teeth, stand up and walk to the van. Otherwise, Albert will have to carry you. You don't want that, do you?"

"Don't want to go to hospital. Want to go home."

"I don't want to go to the hospital, either," Hannah agreed, "but we have to. The doctors need to look at your arm."

"Want King David," Susanna whimpered as she allowed her mother to help her to her feet. "I want David. Now!"

"*Ne,* daughter," Hannah said. "David has to stay here. His belly doesn't feel good."

"Rudy, you wait here for your brother and David," Rebecca instructed. "Bring them to the picnic area and make sure that David isn't separated from the rest of you."

Quickly, the group moved down the walkway to the parking lot where Albert helped Susanna into the backseat of the van and Hannah got in beside her. Grace, Johanna and the children unloaded the lunch baskets while Hannah fastened Susanna's seat belt. Susanna was still crying, but not so frantically.

After making certain that all the children and adults were accounted for and out of the way, Albert drove the short distance to the hospital emergency room.

Once they got Susanna inside, Albert was aware that they attracted a lot of curious stares, but whether it was because of Susanna and Hannah's Amish clothing or Susanna's renewed wailing, he wasn't sure. Susanna's injury was quickly assessed, and they took seats in the waiting room. Albert had assumed that Susanna would calm down, but she continued to cry and to ask for David.

"I'm so sorry, Albert," Hannah said between Susanna's wails. "You planned a fun day for us, and then this had to happen."

He shrugged. "I'm just glad I'm here to help."

"Please stop, Susanna," Hannah coaxed, turning back to her daughter. "There's a soda machine. I'll buy you a soda if you stop crying."

"Want my David!" Fresh tears commenced.

Hannah sighed and glanced away, obviously unsure what to do.

"Maybe I should go back and get him," Albert suggested. "I can always take him back to the park if it doesn't help."

Hannah hesitated, and then nodded. "Maybe you should." She turned to Susanna. "Do you hear that? Albert's going to go get David and bring him here. But if you keep crying, you'll make him cry. And you know his belly hurts when he's upset."

Susanna clamped her lips and her eyelids tightly shut, but tears kept seeping down her face, and she was trembling all over. Hannah looked at Albert. "She's always like this when she hurts herself, even a stubbed toe. She has a difficult time adjusting to pain."

"Want my David," Susanna repeated, eyes still shut. "Want David."

They were still in the waiting room when Albert returned to the emergency room half an hour later with David. The young man seemed nervous, but also eager to be with Susanna. Albert found much of David's speech hard to understand, but the one word he did get, repeated over and over, was Susanna's name.

People twisted their necks to stare as David lumbered across the waiting room to where Susanna sat, but he didn't see them. His gaze was locked on her. Hannah got up and waved him to the seat beside Susanna.

Albert waited to see what David would do. If he'd made an error in judgment, they might have two frightened, adult-size kids to deal with. But just the opposite happened. David took a hold of Susanna's hand and spoke to her, and she opened her eyes. A quavering half smile lit her face as she pointed to her arm. "It hurts," she said and sniffed.

David pulled a large blue paisley handkerchief out of his pocket and held it out to Susanna.

"Blow," he ordered. She did. "Don't cry, Susanna. The d…doctor will make it all better."

"He will?" Susanna handed back the handkerchief.

David nodded, found a clean corner and wiped her wet cheek. "I'm s…sorry you hurt bad."

She nodded, sniffed and gave a small sound of agreement.

"My *dat* said 'No…no crying.' And he bought m…me ice cream." David held up his thumb to show a faint white scar. "Th…three stitches. Three." He held up three fingers to emphasize his point.

*"Ya."* Susanna nodded again. "He sewed it up." Her lower lip quivered. "I don't want the doctor to sew my arm."

"He won't," Hannah assured her. "First they will take a picture of it, and then they'll fix it so it can't move until it's all healed."

David leaned close to wipe a dirty spot on Susanna's chin. "I g…got your feather," he said, pulling a much-the-worse-for-wear green feather out of his other pocket. "F…found it on the ground."

Susanna clutched at the bent and wrinkled parrot feather and smiled. "You found it."

Hannah came to stand by Albert, watching David and Susanna. "The wind blew it out of her hand and she was running after it when she tripped and fell down the steps," she explained.

David and Susanna had their heads together whispering. Susanna's tears had subsided. "They seem very fond of one another," Albert mused aloud. "And David is good for her."

*"Ya,"* Hannah agreed with a sigh. "He is. And I think that they care for each other very much."

Albert nodded. "So maybe…"

"Maybe I've been wrong," she said, softly. "Very wrong. Maybe David is what God planned for Susanna all along."

Albert looked down at Hannah. "You think you're ready to let her marry?"

"Well, I didn't say that." She grimaced. "I still think I'll need a little time." She looked up at him, her eyes moist. "Would that be so terrible? To let them be husband and wife? They couldn't live alone, but they could live with me. With us," she dared.

"I think that might be the perfect solution." He smiled, feeling a tenderness in his heart he'd never felt before. "Maybe the answer to your prayers."

"Have you lost what little sense you ever had?" Martha crossed her arms, jutted one angular hip and scowled at Hannah.

It was Friday morning, nearly a week after Susanna had broken her arm at the zoo. Hannah had seen her sister-in-law at church the day after Susanna's accident, but they'd had no opportunity to have a private conversation. Hannah had been inspecting her peach trees for signs of insect infestation when Martha marched down the lane that led from her home to Hannah's farm.

"Good morning, Martha."

"I shudder to think what my brother would make of this. If you ever gave a minute's consideration to what he would want," Martha shook an admonishing finger. "Poor Jonas. You should be ashamed of yourself, Hannah. I saw Fannie at Fifer's Orchard and she told me that you and that Mennonite are courting. A Mennonite!"

Hannah stiffened. "*Ya,* Martha, we are." And then, instantly, the realization hit her that Reuben must not have discussed any of this with her. That was a shock. She didn't think Reuben kept anything from his wife.

"You're going to leave the church, aren't you? I knew it," she insisted, before Hannah could get in a word. "First Leah and now you. But she was never baptized into the faith. You were, Hannah. You'll be shunned if you turn Mennonite." Her face was getting redder by the second. "You know what this means. Your own daughters and grandchildren won't be able to eat at the same table with you. All of your friends, your neighbors will have to—"

"Albert has petitioned to convert," Hannah cut in.

It only took Martha a moment to pick up steam again. "That's the silliest thing I've ever heard. Albert can't be Amish. What makes him think he can be Amish? He wasn't raised Amish, he was raised Mennonite."

As Martha went on, blood pulsed at Hannah's temples. She wanted to say awful things to Martha—to ask her why she always felt compelled to interfere in other people's private lives, why she had to approach every conversation with such criticism. But she took a deep breath and interrupted again, "Albert wants to become Amish. It's what I want, too."

"I know you think I'm a busybody, that I constantly look for fault in others, but I do care for you, Hannah. Believe it or not, I do. And I care very much what happens to you and your family." Martha's face took on a pinched expression and her lips paled. "I'll admit that I'm too outspoken and that I've harbored jealousy against you in the past. It's not something I'm proud of, but it's true." Tears suddenly filled Martha's eyes. "You don't know how difficult it's been to watch each of your girls make wonderful marriages while my Dorcas sits at home growing older and older."

Hannah stared at her sister-in-law for a moment. She was speechless. Had Martha truly just admitted such a thing? And suddenly Hannah's heart ached for her bristly sister-in-law.

She crossed the short distance between them and wrapped her arms around Martha. For a moment, Martha stood stick-straight, and then Hannah felt a tremor pass through her and she sagged against her, awkwardly returning the hug.

"I'm sorry for the discord I've sowed. It's always been my biggest fault, one I've struggled with since I was a child, but you don't understand how it was for me growing up," Martha said. "My mother was never the kind of mother you've been. Jonas was always her favorite. Jezzy, me, my sisters, we were only girls when my parents needed sons to work the farm."

"*Actch,* Martha, hush now." Hannah rubbed Martha's back. "I'm sure that's not true."

"None of us were ever pretty, but Jonas didn't seem to notice or care. He loved us anyway. Then he met you. Pretty, smart, capable Hannah. Then he was too busy to come by and share jokes or spend time with me."

"Jonas loved you very much," Hannah said. "I never heard him say an unkind word about you or his mother."

"He was like that. He always saw the good in people." Martha disengaged herself and smoothed her faded dress. "But I was born more like Mother. And for better or worse, I speak my mind."

"I've not always been as good a sister by marriage as I should have," Hannah said. "And I admit that if we've clashed at times, I was probably at fault as much as you."

"I'd like to tell myself that, but I doubt it's true," Martha scoffed. "I didn't like the freedom you gave your girls, letting them sashay around the countryside with young men. It wasn't the way I was raised. But it doesn't seem to have hurt any of them. They've all made decent marriages and live according to the *Ordnung*. Maybe if I'd given Dorcas more leeway," she fretted, "she'd have found a fellow when she was eighteen, rosy-cheeked, and sweeter-natured."

"It isn't too late for Dorcas. She's a good girl, a hard worker."

"And where are the young men beating a trail to our door? There's none in Kent County who've shown her more than a passing glance."

"Then maybe you should look farther afield. There are other conservative communities with lots of respectable candidates." Hannah thought for a moment. "You know, your cousin Sara has been very successful in making good matches. If you're concerned about Dorcas, maybe you should talk to Sara."

"And where's her fee to come from? My Reuben was laid up with his broken leg. We had medical bills. We've no extra money to spend on matchmakers." Martha's tone was brittle, but Hannah

knew that finances were often a real problem for
Reuben and Martha.

"Not all the families of the girls provide the fee.
Sara said that just as often, it's the boy's family,
and with a widower, it's usually the case. As he's
more established and getting a younger wife, he's
expected to assume the expense."

"So I'm to put my daughter up for some old
man to bid on?"

Hannah allowed herself a smile. "Dorcas would
have the right to refuse any match she didn't want.
Sara's client Ellie did just that with the young man
they came to consider. He was willing, but she
didn't think he was right for her."

Martha eyed her. "Ellie, the…*short* girl?"

*"Ya."* Hannah smiled to herself. "It's just a suggestion, Martha. Could it hurt to discuss it with
Dorcas?"

"I suppose not, but what would Reuben say?
He's a proud man. Not right to say about a
preacher, but they're only human, too. He sets
some store by our Dorcas. I think it would suit
him if she never married and stayed home to care
for us in our old age."

"Easier for Reuben perhaps, but would it be
right for Dorcas? I've struggled with much the
same thought with Susanna. And I think I've been
holding on to her too tightly. She and David King,
they care for each other deeply."

"You think I don't know that? Saw it months ago. Those two are smitten, all right." Martha set her hands on her hips. "He's a good match for Susanna. David is a decent boy. He was born with troubles, but so was our Susanna. Together, they make up for some of what they lack. And in God's eyes, they're His creations, not ours."

Hannah blinked in surprise. "You would approve of me letting Susanna walk out with David?"

"Why not? Isn't that what the Bible tells us? It's the natural order of things. They should court and then marry. And the sooner the better, I say." Martha drew herself up like a banty hen. "You surprise me Hannah, for all your modern ways. Why doesn't Susanna have as much right to marry as Rebecca did? Of course if they have children, then you and David's mother would have to help—"

"No babies," Hannah said quietly. "David can't father children. Sadie assured me of that."

Martha opened her arms. "There you go, then. I'd say the decision's been made. You should have the banns read as soon as possible. The two of them are innocents now, but they're better married than not. Safer for them both."

"You're right," Hannah agreed, still completely surprised by Martha's view. "It took me a long time to realize that." She looked up. "But after a decent time of courting, I should allow her to marry him if she still wants to."

"*Gut.* That's sensible." Martha looked into her eyes with eyes that had once been as blue as Jonas'. "So why can't you show the same good sense where Albert is concerned?"

Hannah took a step back. "We're not going to argue again, are we?"

"It took a lot for me to come here and bare my faults to you," Martha said. "You owe me the decency of considering what I have to say. It's meant in the best way. Honestly, Hannah. If the congregation did accept Albert, if he did become one of us—and I say *if,* because I doubt the elders would ever approve—how long would your marriage last before he began to regret his decision? Albert would have to turn his back on worldly things—his motor vehicle, his television, his cell phone. You're kidding yourself if you think that such a marriage could ever work."

"I converted for Jonas. I gave up my family and my life for his, and I've never regretted it, not for a single day."

"But you were just a young girl. It's not the same for a man. Not a man his age, set in his ways. You're making a mistake, and that mistake will threaten the stability of our community and your family. He may be a good man, Hannah, but he isn't Amish and he can never be. And for you to ask him to do this for you, why it's just plain selfish."

# Chapter Sixteen

*"Selfish...just plain selfish..."* Martha's words echoed again and again in Hannah's head as she moved through her day. She tried to keep busy. She cleaned off the back porch. She washed strawberries, and then made a shortcake. She tried not to second-guess herself.

But the seeds of doubt, once sown, found fertile ground to grow. Was Martha right? Was she being selfish? Had she run roughshod over what should have been common sense? Was she allowing Albert to make sacrifices that he would later regret? And worst of all, would a marriage with Albert end in unhappiness for both of them?

She never expected to hear good advice from Martha, but she'd never thought to hear her sister-in-law admit jealousy or interfering in other people's lives, either. Could there be threads of truth in what Martha had said about Albert?

From there, the "whys" set in. Why had she allowed her friendship with Albert to become love? Once she'd realized that his feelings for her were growing, why hadn't she rejected further advances? Instead, she'd welcomed them, lain awake thinking of Albert like a lovesick girl. And now they'd taken their case to the elders. It was all in motion. What if Bishop Atlee approved? It was a possibility. Then what? Did Albert truly understand how different his life with her would be?

There was no divorce among the Amish. The sacred bonds of marriage were for life. What if she married Albert and then they found that they had made a terrible mistake? The fault would be hers because she knew all too well the vast divide between the English world and those who practiced the conservative faith of the Amish. Was Martha right? Was she allowing her own selfishness to threaten Albert's future happiness?

Her doubts troubled her so badly that she didn't go outside to meet Albert that evening when he came to tend the alpacas. She barely spoke to Susanna during supper, and went to bed early, but hardly slept a wink. The next morning, she awoke as confused as she'd been when she'd finished her nightly prayers. She found an excuse to go to Miriam's and Ruth's house just as Albert's truck pulled off the blacktop into her lane.

Grace stopped by at midday to invite her and

Susanna to share the evening meal. "John's already invited Uncle Albert. I'm making my famous spaghetti sauce." But Hannah begged off, giving the excuse that she had a headache, which was true. And Susanna couldn't go because she'd already accepted an invitation to eat with the Kings.

Sunday morning, Irwin did the feeding, and since Sundays were always busy, it was easy for her to be absent when Albert came that night. Hannah had never considered herself a coward, but she felt like one now. Did she just need to go to Albert and tell him her fears?

She prayed for guidance, but the answer eluded her.

Was she making a terrible mistake? Would she hurt Albert less if she put an end to this entire courtship now, before worse happened? Had she put her happiness ahead of what was right for Albert, her family, her community? How was she going to talk to Albert about this? What was she going to say to him?

Monday morning she was still fretting over how to tell Albert her fears when he drove into the yard, pulled his truck up to her back porch and knocked on her door. "Hannah," he called. "Come out, or I'm coming in."

She stood in the kitchen, her heart racing in her

chest. She glanced at Susanna. "Please go upstairs and change the sheets on the beds."

"Albert's knocking," Susanna said.

Hannah touched her head nervously, making certain that her *kapp* was in place. Her knees felt weak. "Please, Susanna, the beds. We need to put the sheets into the wash."

Susanna trudged off, but not before Albert pushed open the screen door. "Are you coming out or—"

"I'm coming, Albert."

He held the door for Hannah and she stepped out onto the porch. Two red hens had escaped from the chicken yard and found their way inside the picket fence that enclosed the back of the house. Clouds of dust flew up as they scratched at her marigolds in search of bugs. Ordinarily, she would have chased the chickens, but now she couldn't summon the energy.

Albert took her arm as they descended the steps. "You've been avoiding me. Are you going to tell me why?"

He sounded hurt, and she inwardly winced. The last thing she wanted to do was to hurt him. "I wasn't avoiding you," she hedged. "I've been busy. We've both been busy."

"Hannah." He stepped in front of her. "We've always been honest with one another. I haven't seen you or talked to you since Friday morning.

What's wrong? Have I done something? Have I said something that's upset you?"

Shame flooded her. *"Ya,"* she admitted. "I have been avoiding you." She rested her hand on the gate. It wasn't white like the pickets, but a soft, robin's-egg-blue, a foolish color for a gate, but Susanna had wanted it. And Hannah had to admit that she found herself smiling whenever it caught her eye. Now, her fingers brushed the top rail. "I have been struggling, Albert." She closed her eyes for just an instant before opening them and looking up into that kind, gentle face. Again it struck her how handsome his eyes were, how full of life and compassion. *You're a good man,* she thought. *It wouldn't be fair of me to—*

Albert took hold of her shoulders. "Tell me. What's happened to make you so sad? You can tell me anything. Have you received an answer from the bishop? Has he turned down my request to join the church?"

She shook her head as moisture clouded her vision. "I can't marry you," she blurted.

She heard him catch his breath.

"It's not fair to you," she told him.

"What do you mean, not fair to me?" He dropped his hands to take hers and held them as he gazed deeply into her eyes. "I love you, Hannah. Can you tell me that you don't return that love?"

Her throat constricted so that it became impossible to speak.

"Say it," he insisted. "If that's it, say that you don't love me, and I'll walk away."

She couldn't, because she *did* love him. It didn't matter that their lives were half over or that she was a mother and a grandmother. She loved Albert, and she wanted to spend the rest of her life with him…but she couldn't ask him to make the sacrifice for her. "It's because I *do* love you," she murmured. "That's why I can't marry you. It would be wrong of me to force you to join my church, to give up everything for me. I've been selfish to think that—"

"Oh, Hannah, is that what all this is about? That you think you're asking too much of me?" A genuine smile of relief and joy spread across his face. "You love me? You really do?"

She nodded, looking down at their feet. "*Ya*, Albert. I'm afraid I do, but—"

"No buts. Listen to me. You don't get to decide what's best for me. I'm not one of your children. We're both adults, here, Hannah. Marrying you, becoming Amish, it's what I want, what will bring me peace of mind. Happiness. It's like coming home, Hannah. And that's what I want to do, come home to you, every day."

"But, what if they say you have to give up being a veterinarian? It's all you've ever wanted."

"It's not all I've *ever* wanted. I've wanted some-one like you. You're a gift from God to me, and maybe, just maybe, I'm a gift to you from God. That's more important than how I live or what I do for a living."

*A gift from God.* Albert's words cut through her despair like sunshine through dark clouds. Without thinking, she stepped closer to Albert, slipped her arms around his neck, and rose on tiptoes to kiss him full on the mouth. And then, as if it were the most natural thing in the world, Albert's arms were around her, and he was kiss-ing her back, a tender, sweet kiss full of promise and the thrill of two hearts beating to a single note.

Albert's lips were firm and warm, and they fit hers perfectly. They kept kissing, standing there, wrapped in each other's arms in the full light of day.

Which is exactly where Samuel, her son-in-law, the deacon of her church and enforcer of proper behavior found them. "Hannah! Albert!"

They broke apart, shocked at being caught, laughing, and as silly as any two kids caught in a similar situation.

"Kissing?" Samuel attempted his sternest dea-con tone, but Hannah detected a hint of disguised humor.

"I'm afraid so," she admitted. "You see, Samuel. We love each other, and it would be better for the family and our community if you would allow us to be together in holy matrimony."

"Better than continuing to cause a scandal," Albert supplied. She glanced at him. He winked, and she had to stifle a giggle. She had lost her mind. Truly. But it was all she could do to keep both feet on the ground and give her son-in-law the respect he deserved while her lips were still deliciously tingling from Albert's kiss.

"Hmmph." Samuel's expression grew serious. "That's exactly why I'm here. To talk to you. Bishop Atlee and the elders have come to a decision." He hesitated. "Are you prepared to abide by it?"

Albert reached for her hand, captured it and held it tightly. "We are."

*"Ya,"* Hannah agreed. "We are."

*"Gut.* Then we start at the same place." Samuel clasped his hands. "Bishop Atlee has prayed for guidance, as have Reuben and Caleb and I. Yours is a very unusual request, but then we think you two are unusual people." He broke into a smile. "You know of course that it's our tradition that a man or woman may ask to join our congregation only once he or she lives as Amish for one year."

Hannah's rush of happiness smacked into the solid wall of the realization that they would have to wait an entire year to be together. A year? She wanted to have the banns read tomorrow. But the *Ordnung* was the *Ordnung*. The elders' word was law. She glanced up at Albert, reading both the joy and the disappointment of having to wait lingering there.

"I understand," Albert said.

"But we believe your case is special," Samuel went on. "You are not English, and Anna has told me that your grandparents were born Amish, and that you share our history and traditions."

Albert nodded. "My father's people."

"Bishop Atlee and I discussed these special conditions, and he believes that you would know your heart and God's will in six months' time."

"Six months!" Hannah was unable to cover her excitement.

"Now, it's customary for a convert to live among us and as one of us for that time," Samuel continued. "So Anna and I would like to offer our home as that haven."

"Thank you," Albert said. "I'd consider it an honor."

Hannah was too full of joy to speak. Albert would be there, just across the pasture. If he lived with Samuel and Anna, no one would question that he fulfilled his promise. The tears that had threatened overflowed and wet her cheeks.

"Now, we expect you to give Hannah a proper

courtship under the eyes of her family and community. You will come to our worship services and share in our work frolics and holidays. You will be part of my family, Albert." Mischief twinkled in Samuel's eyes. "And you will have to dress Amish. Plain."

"I can do that," Albert said.

"Remember, marrying Hannah may be your goal, but it isn't a reason to convert to our faith. Conversion must be heartfelt. It must be genuine. And if you feel that it isn't right for you, you must be brave enough to admit it," Samuel continued.

Again, Albert nodded. "I understand."

"Good." Samuel folded his arms over his broad chest and grinned. "It's settled. But there will be no more kissing until after the marriage. Is that clear?"

"*Ya,* Samuel," Hannah said. "No more kissing."

"We'll try," Albert promised. "But it won't be easy."

"There is one more stipulation that is most unusual, but I think you'll find a way to make it work," Samuel said. "Bishop Atlee doesn't want you to waste your veterinary skills. Our community depends on you too much. You can continue to use your motor vehicle to care for your animal patients, but you'll have to hire a driver to take you to and from the office. Or have your nephew transport you. When you're not working we'll expect you to use a horse and buggy. Is that clear?"

"He can still practice?" Hannah asked. "That's wonderful."

"And why not? We follow tradition, but we are not inflexible. As Bishop Atlee says, 'It would be a sin to waste the skills that the Lord has given him.'"

Hannah turned to face Albert and for a moment, it was as if Samuel wasn't standing there. "Albert, we're getting married," she murmured.

His smile filled her heart with joy. "We're getting married, Hannah."

# *Epilogue*

Six months to the day that Albert first dressed in traditional Old Order clothing, Bishop Atlee baptized him into the faith. The community welcomed Albert with open arms, and two weeks later, Samuel announced the intent of couples Albert Hartman and Hannah Yoder, and David King and Susanna Yoder to join in holy matrimony on the second Tuesday of February. The publishing of their banns launched Hannah into a frenzy of preparation: sewing, house cleaning, compiling a guest list and handwriting invitations.

The weeks between the announcement and the ceremony flew by, and almost before Hannah could catch her breath, she found herself standing beside Albert in front of the bishop, surrounded by family, neighbors and friends in Samuel and Anna's parlor. "Are the two of you prepared to enter marriage according to God's word?" Bishop Atlee asked.

"*Ya,* I am," Hannah said, her response nearly drowned out by Albert's deep and heartfelt assent. Her heart raced; she felt giddy with excitement. All the troubling doubts had evaporated, leaving her with a feeling of peace and anticipation.

"Albert, are you certain that this is the woman that God has chosen to be your wife?"

He squeezed her hand. "I am."

"And you, Hannah," the bishop continued. "Are you certain in the deepest part of your heart and mind that Albert is the man that God has chosen for you?"

"I am."

Bishop Atlee's beard was as white as the snowflakes that softly fell against the tall windows, and his eyes sparkled with affection. He looked to Hannah like some prophet from the Old Testament as he spoke the familiar words. "And do you both promise to cherish and sustain each other in sickness and in health according to God's laws, and to remain as one so long as you both shall live?"

"I do," they said together. And with that, the bishop nodded and motioned them back to their seats on the bench.

"David and Susanna?" the bishop said.

Susanna looked at her mother and Hannah smiled, fighting tears. "Go on," she whispered.

Hand in hand David and Susanna made their

way to the bishop and repeated the same words Hannah and Albert had just exchanged. Their speech might not have been as clear and they stumbled over some words, but no one present could have doubted the love that shone in David's and Susanna's eyes. And before Hannah knew it, the couple was seated beside her. Two hymns and a final prayer concluded the ceremony, and then everyone rose and helped to rearrange the chairs so that the men could carry in tables for the wedding feast.

Charley and Eli directed the creation of a special table for the bridal parties. Women quickly covered the surface with white tablecloths, added plates, glasses and silverware, and adorned the *eck* with a large pewter bowl of fruit. Hannah had eyes only for Albert, with a few motherly glances at Susanna. Her precious youngest daughter glowed with an inner light, seemingly so overcome with happiness at finally having her new bridegroom, David, that she refused to let go of his hand, and couldn't stop talking. David seemed equally ecstatic, but rather than bubble over with excitement, he simply grinned, nodded and stared at Susanna as if he was afraid that she might disappear at any moment.

At last, guests and bridal party were all in their places, Hannah and Albert to the left of the corner, Susanna and David to the right, both couples flanked by their attendants—Anna, Grace, Samuel and John on Hannah's side and Rebecca, Ruth, Eli and Caleb on Susanna's. Seated along the walls were the rest of the family and honored guests, including Sara and Ellie, who was moving to Seven Poplars.

"Finally," Albert whispered to Hannah as volunteers began to carry in platters of roast turkey, ham, fried chicken and sausage. "I'm starving."

"Aren't you always?" Hannah teased, thinking how handsome he looked in his plain black coat and trousers and starched white shirt. For just a second, she closed her eyes and savored the joy of God's love. How blessed she was to have this new beginning with this strong and caring man at her side.

"And why wouldn't I be?" Albert asked, reaching for her hand and squeezing it, pulling her out of her reverie. "This getting married stuff is hard work."

She nodded and smiled back at him. He was her husband and now the head of her house. It seemed right, and she was content, so content that she had resigned her position as schoolteacher and planned to stay home and take care of him, and Susanna and David. "No regrets?" she whispered to Albert.

"At leaving Samuel and Anna's house, and her

pie, now that we're wed?" Mischief lurked in his dark eyes. "Well, maybe just a little. Her apple-cranberry—"

Hannah laughed.

"Ah, look what's coming now." Girls carried mountains of sweet potatoes, mashed potatoes, egg noodles, rice and vegetables of all kinds, followed by boys with woven baskets of yeast breads, hot rolls and biscuits.

Samuel rose from his place at the table and asked for a moment of silent grace before the meal began. Heads bowed, and peace descended on the house, a quiet broken only by the rustle of the wind through the eaves and the soft patter of snowflakes against the windowpanes. Albert didn't let go of Hannah's hand and she was secretly proud that he didn't care if people saw them. The prayer ended and everyone began to eat.

Hannah had just taken a slice of turkey on her plate when Albert's cell phone rang. Eyes widened. Heads turned. Neighbor's craned their necks to see who had brought a forbidden phone to the wedding supper.

Albert took the small flip phone from his pocket. "Sorry," he called. Whispers and amused glances rippled around the room. As a veterinarian, he had received special dispensation from the bishop to carry his cell phone with him. He stood up and pushed the button. "Hello." A nod, and then, to Hannah's surprise, he handed the phone to her. "It's for you."

"For me?" She stared in surprise. "Who would be calling me?"

Albert laughed. "It's my wedding gift to you. I'd hoped it would be here today, but it seems it's arriving tomorrow."

Nervously, Hannah rose, bringing the cell phone to her ear. "Hello?"

*"Mam?"* Leah! It was Leah, the only daughter not here with her today! *"Mam!* It's me," Leah said. "The baby and I are coming home for a long visit. Albert bought us a plane ticket."

Hannah's heart leaped. "You're coming home?" The phone slipped from numb fingers as she threw her arms around Albert's neck and kissed him full on the mouth.

Laughing, he caught her by the waist and lifted her up, kissing her so hard that her *kapp* slid halfway off her head. Hannah didn't care. All that mattered was the love that welled up inside her and the warm shouts of approval from those who mattered most in her life. "You wonderful, wonderful man!" she exclaimed. "I love you!"

"And I love you," Albert replied. And then he kissed her again, his strong embrace and tender caress making her feel like a young bride and fill-ing her heart to overflowing with the sweet joy of God's abundant grace.

* * * * *

Dear Reader,

Hello, I'm so pleased to see you. Come in. I've been making strawberry jam today. Won't you sit down and join me for a cup of coffee and a buttermilk biscuit with warm jam? It's always nice to have company. Wait, let me clear away my knitting. I'm making a bonnet for my daughter Miriam. She's expecting a blessing before Christmas, and we're all so happy for her. New babies are such a joy.

This big farmhouse has echoed with the laughter of so many babies, and I hope it will continue on that way for many years to come. Something new and exciting is always happening in such a big family, but we're happy to welcome old friends and make new ones. Our community is a loving one bound by tradition and a love of God. We worship together, celebrate weddings and baptisms, and come together when we suffer losses and pain.

Those of you who have visited with me before have watched my daughters find true love and marriage, but I never expected it to happen to me again. I'm constantly reminded of life's unexpected blessings. And don't think that because I've found husbands for my girls that there aren't a few surprises still coming to Seven Poplars. Romance has a way of blossoming here as it does wherever there are willing hearts. So please come back and join us soon. There's always an extra place at the table for you.

Wishing you peace and joy.
*Hannah* (via Emma Miller)

## Questions for Discussion

1. Did Hannah overreact when she realized Susanna was missing from the house? Do you think Hannah handled the situation well, or should she have done something differently?

2. Why do you think Hannah agreed to allow Albert to bring the alpacas to her farm?

3. Albert took Hannah's hand at the restaurant. If you had been Hannah, how would you have handled the situation?

4. Do you think Albert fit in with Hannah's family, even though he was not a part of the Amish community?

5. Were you surprised by David and Susanna's behavior at Rebecca's wedding? Was Albert right to tell Hannah?

6. Do you think Hannah's response to Susanna's rebellion was reasonable? What would you have done if she had been your daughter?

7. What do you think attracted Albert to Hannah, and Hannah to Albert? Is their attraction

to each other a good foundation for a later-in-life marriage?

8. Hannah finally decided to allow Susanna to walk out with David. What made Hannah change her mind? Was Albert's opinion on the matter helpful?

9. Albert decides to become Amish. Did you feel he was abandoning his faith?

10. Were you surprised by Bishop Atlee's decision? Where do you think Albert and Hannah's relationship will be in five years?

# LARGER-PRINT BOOKS!

**GET 2 FREE**
**LARGER-PRINT NOVELS**
**PLUS 2 FREE**
**MYSTERY GIFTS**

*Love Inspired*
## SUSPENSE
RIVETING INSPIRATIONAL ROMANCE

### Larger-print novels are now available...

**YES!** Please send me 2 FREE LARGER-PRINT Love Inspired® Suspense novels and my 2 FREE mystery gifts (gifts are worth about $10). After receiving them, if I don't wish to receive any more books, I can return the shipping statement marked "cancel." If I don't cancel, I will receive 4 brand-new novels every month and be billed just $5.24 per book in the U.S. or $5.74 per book in Canada. That's a savings of at least 23% off the cover price. It's quite a bargain! Shipping and handling is just 50¢ per book in the U.S. and 75¢ per book in Canada.* I understand that accepting the 2 free books and gifts places me under no obligation to buy anything. I can always return a shipment and cancel at any time. Even if I never buy another book, the two free books and gifts are mine to keep forever.

110/310 IDN F5CC

Name _____ (PLEASE PRINT) _____

Address _____ Apt. # _____

City _____ State/Prov. _____ Zip/Postal Code _____

Signature (if under 18, a parent or guardian must sign)

**Mail to the Harlequin® Reader Service:**
**IN U.S.A.:** P.O. Box 1867, Buffalo, NY 14240-1867
**IN CANADA:** P.O. Box 609, Fort Erie, Ontario L2A 5X3

**Are you a current subscriber to Love Inspired Suspense books
and want to receive the larger-print edition?
Call 1-800-873-8635 or visit www.ReaderService.com.**

* Terms and prices subject to change without notice. Prices do not include applicable taxes. Sales tax applicable in N.Y. Canadian residents will be charged applicable taxes. Offer not valid in Quebec. This offer is limited to one order per household. Not valid for current subscribers to Love Inspired Suspense larger-print books. All orders subject to credit approval. Credit or debit balances in a customer's account(s) may be offset by any other outstanding balance owed by or to the customer. Please allow 4 to 6 weeks for delivery. Offer available while quantities last.

**Your Privacy**—The Harlequin® Reader Service is committed to protecting your privacy. Our Privacy Policy is available online at www.ReaderService.com or upon request from the Harlequin Reader Service.

We make a portion of our mailing list available to reputable third parties that offer products we believe may interest you. If you prefer that we not exchange your name with third parties, or if you wish to clarify or modify your communication preferences, please visit us at www.ReaderService.com/consumerchoice or write to us at Harlequin Reader Service Preference Service, P.O. Box 9062, Buffalo, NY 14269. Include your complete name and address.

LISLPDIR13R